DANIEL T. REESE
AND THE
PROPHET
KING

DANIEL T. REESE AND THE PROPHET KING

JESSE EDWARD CORRALEZ

DANIEL T. REESE AND THE PROPHET KING

This is a work of fiction. All of the characters, names, incidents, organizations, and dialogue in this novel are either the products of the author's imagination or are used fictitiously.

iUniverse books may be ordered through booksellers or by contacting:

iUniverse
1663 Liberty Drive
Bloomington, IN 47403
www.iuniverse.com
1-800-Authors (1-800-288-4677)

Because of the dynamic nature of the Internet, any web addresses or links contained in this book may have changed since publication and may no longer be valid. The views expressed in this work are solely those of the author and do not necessarily reflect the views of the publisher, and the publisher hereby disclaims any responsibility for them.

Any people depicted in stock imagery provided by Thinkstock are models, and such images are being used for illustrative purposes only. Certain stock imagery © Thinkstock.

ISBN: 978-1-5320-2359-0 (sc)
ISBN: 978-1-5320-2360-6 (e)

Print information available on the last page.

iUniverse rev. date: 06/23/2017

CHAPTER 1

August 2016

"Come on, Danny. Come on. Give it a shot. You can do it, dude," hollered Daniel T. Reese's pal, Joey Nape.

They were two of half-a-dozen preteens out in a cul-de-sac trying to outdo each other on skateboards.

"It's easy, Danny. Just roll out, jump on, and lean back on your rear foot. The board will kick up, and then you guide it up and over the curb."

This was taking place in a neighborhood in the city of Vancouver, Washington. Just across the mighty Columbia River from Portland, Oregon. Daniel T. Reese and Joey Nape were both twelve.

Their summer vacation from school was in its seventh week, and Daniel was destined to miss a large part of what remained—with his pal Joey, that is.

"Come on, Danny! It's a no brainier, man. Do it. Do it," Joey said, egging him on.

"OK, OK, Joey. Shut up already," said Daniel T. with his left foot on the front of his board. Using his right foot, he pushed off into a rollout on the street asphalt and aimed for the curb.

A little too far out, he placed his right foot at the rear of the board, leaned back, and the front of the board shot up. Daniel did not know what to do next. He shifted his weight slightly, and the front of his board plopped back down onto the front wheels. The board struck the side of the curb hard, throwing Daniel T. up in the air. He did a half twist and came down on the sidewalk on his back, where his head whiplashed against the cement with a thud.

At the local hospital, where Daniel T. was rushed by ambulance, doctors did a thorough examination: X-rays, CT scan, and MRI. They found nothing but a goose-egg lump on the back of his head. A little shaving and three stitches would fix that. His breathing was good; his blood pressure was normal, and his heart rate was fine. All of his vital signs were OK, but Daniel T. Reese was in a deep coma.

"Whoa," said Danny as he awoke suddenly. "Where am I?" He was flat on his back on hard-packed ground.

"You are nearly in the middle of the street," a deep voice told him. "You should move out of the way quickly or be run over by that donkey and wagon coming toward you."

Daniel got up on his elbows and looked to his right and saw nothing but pedestrians. Then he heard something and looked to his left.

"Yau!" he yelped and rolled out of the way just in time.

"Good move, boy," the voice said.

Daniel hoisted himself upright and took a good look about him. On both sides of the street were stands of one stature or another with people going to and from them.

"Where am I?" Daniel asked again.

The man who owned the voice, dressed in robes from head to toe, slowly walked around Daniel, looking him up and down and focusing especially upon his footwear.

"You are in Nazareth. Where do you come from? What tribe do you belong to? I have never seen such manner of dress. And on your feet, what is it that you wear?" asked the man.

"Nazareth?" Daniel questioned, totally astonished. "Where is that, dude? Sounds like a place maybe up north in the Seattle area. There's a lot of towns up there with really funked out names. Stuff like Issaquah, Encumclaw, and Snoqualmie. I think they are Indian names, but I'm not all that sure cause I don't belong to a tribe. My shoes? Dude, they are Nike's—the kind Michael Jordan wears, or maybe that is O'Neil. Hey, all of them big ball players wear 'em, man.

"Damn! Sure is hot. Them robes help keep you cool? I notice everyone is wearing 'em. And, yo, dude, did you score your wigged-out sandals like at the Walmart?"

The man held up one hand to the boy. "It is hot out here in the sun. Come. Let us find a place in some shade. You seem to enjoy speaking; however, you use a certain manner and tone of voice that I do not recognize. Also, you have many words that are strange, and I do not understand."

The man led Daniel off to a side street or alleyway and found a place beneath a tree.

"What land do you come from? What village? What people?" asked the man.

"Well," said the boy, "I live in Vancouver, Washington in the United States of America. If Nazareth is up north, then you know where that is. My people I guess are European, not exactly sure where, or maybe from Minnesota. My name is Daniel T. Reese. What's yours?"

"Daniel is a good strong name," the man said as he reached out and grasped the boy's offered right hand, but his hand wrapped itself around the boy's wrist, as was the custom in his land.

Daniel smiled big, and he took hold of the man's wrist as well. "Cool, dude," he said and then slid his hand over the man's palm, snapped his fingers, and held up his hand. "Give me five after that slide!"

The man just stood there and glanced at his hand and then at the boy's.

"Aw, man, you be lame. I hold up my hand and you do the same. Go ahead, like this," Daniel pointed to his right hand with his left.

The man held up his right hand.

"All right, dude. Now we cross and strap 'em together." They did. "Cool. Later, I'll teach you more handshake shit. Now, where exactly is Nazareth?" asked Daniel. "I don't know how I got here, but I need to be getting back to Vancouver. How much time has gone by since I was skateboarding with Joel and the guys? Do you know what time it is?"

The man shaded his eyes with one hand as he looked up toward the sun. "I believe that it is close to one," he said.

"Don't you have a watch?"

"Watch what, Daniel?"

"Oh, never mind. Can you point me to the nearest freeway? Maybe I can thumb a ride back home."

"What is a freeway?" asked the man.

"You know, where cars and trucks and buses go one way or another to wherever they want to go," Daniel said.

"What are cars and trucks and buses?"

"Are you serious, dude?" asked an astonished Daniel. "Aw, man, you really don't know, huh? Jesus! Just where am I?" Daniel asked again, furiously this time, as he looked around him.

"Do you know my son?" asked the man with a smile on his face.

"I don't think so," said Daniel, "but maybe. What's his name?"

"You just said it. His name is Jesus and I am Joseph.

CHAPTER 2

"Jesus," repeated Daniel, "that sure isn't a very common name. But I guess it's cool. How old is he?"

"He is twelve, Daniel."

"Yeah? Me too. Maybe he knows where I might be able to get a ride back to Vancouver. How far do you think it is from here, Joseph?"

"I do not know how far because I have no idea where this Vancouver is located. I did not hear of it until you brought it up. Is it maybe toward Egypt? Maybe it lies somewhere near Jerusalem or Bethlehem. Why is it that you do not know where it is? How did you come here to Nazareth? Did you not look upon the way here, Daniel?" said Joseph.

"No, I don't know any of those things you asked," replied Daniel, and then he fell silent for a few moments before saying, "I don't know where I am or how I got here. Will you help me, Joseph? I don't know what to do or where to go. Somehow, I must be far, far away from where I live. I understand you when you talk, but your manner, the way you say words, seems kind of strange. What language is spoken here in Nazareth, Joseph? Where I came from, we speak English. Well, mostly."

"Aramaic is the tongue spoken here—also mostly. And, yes, Daniel, I will help you," Joseph said. "Come. Follow me to my home and meet my family. You will be welcomed by all and may stay for as long as you wish. Maybe in time, we will be able to locate the whereabouts of your Vancouver and a way to get you there."

"Thank you, Joseph. If I speak English and you speak Aramaic, how come we understand each other?"

"Daniel, in your land, you speak your tongue. Since you are here in my land, you are speaking mine. I know that you are because I know the words—the sound of them."

"That's funny, Joseph, because to me, you sound like you are speaking English. Weird, huh? You know, my grandfather says 'far out' when he is expressing, like joy, like that, dude. He told me that there was a singer once named John Denver and that he used to say that a lot. So if I am in a strange land speaking a strange language, err, tongue, it could be far out, huh?" Daniel rattled on as they walked.

"Yes, Daniel, it certainly could be far. Maybe someone here in Nazareth knows where your Vancouver is. If not, perhaps a traveler passing through may know of it. We shall see," Joseph told the boy.

Soon they arrived at Joseph's home. It looked pretty much like all the other buildings in the Nazareth village that Daniel had observed along the way. He thought that they pretty much looked like the American Indian Pueblos he had seen in books. They appeared to be made of mud bricks: adobe, they were called, as he remembered. Inside Joseph's home, sitting at a table, were a woman, a young man of approximately Daniel's age, a younger boy, and a little girl of about seven or so. Daniel right away figured that the older boy must be Jesus.

Joseph, introduce Mary as his wife; their sons, Jesus and James; and their daughter, Salome.

"Daniel," he told them, "has come to us from a very far place called Vancouver. He does not know how he got here. I found him almost in the middle of the street near the marketplace. He was just lying there flat on his back, and it appeared that he had been sleeping and just awakened. His first words were, 'Whoa. Where am I?' Daniel likes to talk, so after our meal, he might tell us about his people and their village." Joseph pulled a stool up to the table for Daniel as he spoke.

"He informed me that in his land, they speak English, and so he and I have no idea how he is able to speak our tongue. Which I pointed out to him that he is certainly doing. He, in turn, told me that it sounds to him that I am speaking his language. Well, it matters not since what is of import is that we understand what we speak to each other."

After their meal, Joseph said he was headed to his workshop, which was located on one side of the house. It was not more than a thatched roof over shallow adobe brick walls on three sides.

"Come join us," he said. "Jesus is my helper. We are carpenters. During your stay with us, perhaps you might like to learn the trade."

"Yes," Jesus said, "come with us. Later, you and I will go and see some of my friends, and you can tell us about the land you came from…this Vancouver. Maybe in time we can figure out how you got here and how to get you back."

"OK," Daniel replied. "I seem to recall something. Something to do with you, Jesus. Not sure exactly what it is, but your name and your father's and mother's names seem somehow familiar. Matter of fact, even Nazareth is starting to sound familiar. Maybe I am in another country, even if I don't know how I got here. But maybe I have been here before and am starting to remember."

"Well," Joseph said, "do you remember where you were, what you were doing just before you woke up in the street in the bazaar here in Nazareth?"

By that time, they had walked into Joseph's workshop. Inside, Daniel saw tools that he could easily recognize: handsaws in several sizes and shapes, and chisels also in different shapes and sizes. There were mallets, clamps, and knives as well. There were hand-drawn shavers and sharpeners, two or three adzes, and other tools that Daniel did not recognize or know what they we're used for. The adz he simply placed as an odd-shaped ax.

After having looked all about, he asked, "Don't you have any electric tools, Joseph?"

Joseph looked to Jesus and then replied, "What is an electric tool, Daniel? I believe that I have at least one of every tool for carpentry that has ever been devised. Perhaps electric tools have recently come in from another land, Egypt or Persia, and I have not yet become aware of such. Although, I cannot imagine any other form of tool for carpentry that would make it easier or faster than what I already possess, but please, tell me of these electric tools, Daniel."

"Yes," said Jesus, "do tell us. If there are tools of the trade that will make it faster and easier to accomplish, I, for one, would certainly want them in our shop."

Joseph chuckled and said to his preteen son, "Yes, Jesus, I am certain that you would, since that may lead to more available time for you to gather with your friends to tell tales and get into mischief."

Jesus smiled and hung his head. "Maybe, father, but I was thinking that better tools would allow us more time to make more things to sell at bazaars and enrich our lives."

Joseph reached out and ruffled the boy's hair.

"You are a good son, Jesus, and you deserve more time to be a child. You are now at the brink of manhood and that remaining time will too soon pass. God only knows what is in store for you in the coming years."

Daniel tried his best to explain electric tools but could not get past his very negligible knowledge of electricity. In trying to define electric-powered everything, he got into televisions, radios, clocks, toasters, lamps, and lightbulbs. But, of course, the more that he divulged to Joseph and Jesus about anything and everything electric, the more dumbfounded they seemed to become. Daniel did notice that Jesus seemed to grasp the concept, but he only sat and listened quietly with a calm and peaceful smile gracing his countenance.

CHAPTER 3

"All that you have told us about electrical tools and all those other things, and that electricity makes them work, seems magical, Daniel," Joseph said. "I hope that it is not the doings of bad magic and that your people do not fare badly because of it. Later, you may share more of what makes up your lives in your village of Vancouver. Now, Jesus, you take Daniel and hunt up your friends, and present them to him and him to them. You both may be gone until suppertime."

"Thank you, father," said a smiling Jesus. Then to Daniel he said, "Come. Let's go find Abraham and Joshua and Levi."

Together, Daniel and Jesus made their way from one mud brick house to another until they had collected all three boys. The village of Nazareth was small; it took little time before five twelve- and nearly twelve-year-old grinning lads were together.

"What are you guys smiling at?" asked Daniel.

"Your robes or whatever it is that you are covered with," said Levi. "Does everyone in your village wear that?"

"Well, yes," replied Daniel. "This is a T-shirt," he pointed at his chest. "And these are pants, which, by the way, are named after you, Levi. On my feet are socks." Daniel hiked up his pant legs. "And these are shoes. We also wear something like you dudes have on your feet, like sandals."

"Why were your pants named after me?" asked Levi.

"Hell if I know, man," said Daniel. "What's with those funky-ass robes you all are wearing? I saw that everyone does: men, women, and kids."

The other boys glanced at each other and then Joshua spoke. "I'm sure that none of us know what funky means, but we do know that our robes surely have nothing to do with asses. Why do you bring donkeys into your question?"

"Huh?" Daniel said. "Donkeys? Who's talking about donkeys?"

"You," said Abraham. "You said funky-ass robes."

"Well," replied Daniel, "I wasn't referring to donkeys."

"What then, Daniel? Did you not say ass?" Abraham quizzed.

"Yeah, yes I did, Abe," answered Daniel, "but it was not meant as in donkey."

"No? Then what did you mean?" Abraham asked.

"Well," Daniel stammered, "like in ass—as in badass, wild ass, dumb ass… Shit, man, I don't know. The only thing I know for sure is that this is called an ass." Daniel turned and pointed to his rump. "All other references to ass probably have nothing to do with a person's ass, and I'm not sure about references to donkeys, but there you have it. I guess funky-ass means either cool or not cool. You know what I mean?"

Abraham, Joshua, and Levi said in unison, "No!"

"Aw, man! Forget it," said Daniel. "But I would fit in better if I were dressed like everyone else. All the people here look at me like I'm a freak. I don't have any money, so I can't buy stuff. Do any of you guys know anyone who might trade me funky-ass robes for my far-out Levis and T-shirt? And maybe my fine Nike's for sandals like you all are wearing?"

"Hmm," Joshua said, "I would trade with you, but then everyone would stare at me like I am a…What did you say, Daniel?"

"Freak, dude," Daniel told him.

"Aha, a freak," Joshua said with a serious squint in his eyes. "What is a 'freak,' Daniel?"

"A freak," repeated Daniel T. Reese, "well, heck, I guess you could say that a freak is someone who is different, looks different, and acts different. Yeah, that's a freak, all right."

"Aha!" exclaimed Jesus. "That certainly explains you."

Abraham and Joshua joined Jesus in a laugh.

"Yeah, I guess that is what I am to you guys and everyone else in this land. You guys would be, too, in Vancouver," Daniel said.

"OK," said Abraham, "now we know what freak means, so what does 'dude' mean?"

"Dude means a guy, a man. It's just another way of saying it, like, 'Aw, man.'

Instead, you could say, 'Aw, dude.' Like that," Daniel told them. "And freaky means like being a freak. You could say to a guy, 'Yo, man, you're one freaky dude.' See what I mean?"

Jesus said, "Yes, dude." They all laughed.

Joshua then cut in. "I know a man who barters and trades in everything. Maybe he will trade with you, Daniel."

"Right on, Josh!" retorted Daniel with a happy face.

Before they headed out to find the trader, Levi spoke up. "Daniel, you referred to Abraham as Abe and to Joshua as Josh. Why?"

"Huh?" replied Daniel. "What are you talking about, dude?"

"Their names are Abraham and Joshua," said Levi.

"Yeah, so?"

"You did not use their names, Daniel," Levi told him.

"Sure I did…Oh, I see what you mean," said a grinning Daniel. "Abe is short for Abraham and Josh is short for Joshua. You guys don't use nicknames, huh?"

"What are nicknames?" asked Abraham.

"Nicknames can be a lot of things but mostly part of the name like Abe and Josh. Sometimes what a guy does or looks like will have people using a nickname. Like if a dude loses one leg or arm or finger, he might be nicknamed 'Stumpy.' If a guy limps, he might be called 'Gimpy.' Stuff like that. Some people call me Dan instead of Daniel. You get it?"

"Yes, I think so. What might I be nicknamed?" asked Levi.

Daniel pondered that a moment and then he said, "Well, we could call you 'Lee.'"

"All right," Levi said. "That fits. What about Jesus?"

"Yeah, what about you, Jesus?" Daniel turned to him and asked. "You have not said a single word about this nickname thing. What do you think?"

"Daniel," Jesus said in his soft and gentle voice. "My name is such that it may not be shortened for a nickname but perhaps in time, people will chose to refer to me with words other than my name."

"Like what, Jesus?" asked Abraham.

"Later in life, I wish to travel. Since I am from Nazareth, perhaps some will refer to me as the Nazarene!"

"Hmm, that might happen, dude," Daniel said. "Let's go get me some funky-ass robes.

CHAPTER 4

The trader, Ishmael, a wizened man of about forty or so years and small in stature, was greatly taken by Daniel's Nike shoes. He told the boy to pick out any robes that he liked and some sandals in exchange for the shoes. Daniel was glad to hear that because he didn't really want to lose his Levis and T-shirt.

As the other boys watched, Daniel peeled off his shoes and socks and handed then over to the leering Ishmael. Ish sat down on the ground and pulled off his sandals. He had watched Daniel remove his socks so now he took them and pulled them onto his feet. He and Daniel wore pretty much the same size. Then Daniel showed him how to lace up and tie the Nike's.

Daniel picked out a tan-colored robe and sash, as well as a blue over-robe garment that was sleeveless and worn like an overcoat. The whole outfit would be gathered at the waist with the sash. Daniel slipped on his sandals and pulled the robes over his cloths.

Levi said to him, "Daniel, aren't you going to remove your garments?"

"Huh?" asked Daniel. "Oh, you mean my T-shirt and Levis? Well, I guess that I can, but I want to keep them. I'll roll 'em up and carry them."

He then undid his belt, unzipped his trousers, and pulled them off followed by his T-shirt, which he had to remove his robes to get off.

The boys and Ishmael were amazed at Daniel's undershorts. Daniel saw them staring. "What?" he said. "You guys never saw underwear before? What do you wear under your robes, dudes?"

"Nothing," said Joshua. "What for? We are already covered by our robes."

"Yeah, huh?" Daniel said. "I have wondered about that myself. Oh well, that's the way we do it back home. Force of habit, I guess. I'll leave 'em on."

Then Daniel turned to the trader. "Thank you, Ishmael. Hey, you don't happen to have a skateboard, do you?"

Ishmael squinted his eyes as he looked about his holdings in his hut. "Uh, what is that you ask? What kind of what?"

"A skateboard, dude. You know, a board about so long," said Daniel while extending his hands out from each other about three feet, "and with wheels at each end?"

"No," replied Ishmael. "I have no such thing. What is it used for? It would be too small to carry much of anything."

"It's not for carrying…Well, I guess you can say that it is, because you get on it and roll out," Daniel said."

"But, Daniel," Abraham said, "a board of that length is so small. How wide is it? Wide enough for us to sit upon it?"

"No, no," Daniel told them. "It is only about so wide." He indicated the width with his hands held out about six to seven inches apart. "And you don't sit on it, dudes, you stand. Do you have sidewalks or paved streets anywhere? I don't think a skateboard would work too cool on dirt."

Jesus spoke up. "I do not know what a sidewalk is, but in Jerusalem, the Romans have had some roads and passageways paved with stones."

"Jerusalem? Hey, really guys, where am I?" a quizzical Daniel asked. "You know what? This is getting weirder and weirder. Let me see…hmm, I was skateboarding and messed up, hit the curb with my board, and flew up in the air. Then I hit the sidewalk and…Hey, that's it! I knocked myself out, and all this is just a dream. Yeah, yeah! That's it! OK, I'll just chill out and enjoy it. I'll hang with you guys until I wake up."

"Hang?" exclaimed Levi. "Why should we hang, Daniel, we have not done anything bad or wrong that we should be sentenced to hang."

"Aw, man, I don't mean hang, hang. I mean stay with you until I either wake up back at my home or find a way to get me back there. Where is Nazareth? What state? What country?" Daniel said.

Joshua responded, "Our village, Nazareth, is in Galilee, which is in Palestine. And that is all I know of that. As to what state? Well, I guess I have to say that Nazareth is in a pretty good state. No one is starving, and we all have homes, of one type or another, to live in."

Jesus, Abraham, and Levi nodded in agreement.

Daniel T. regarded them all with a wide grin, and he shook his head and said, "Like John Denver used to say, you dudes are far out. Well, I don't really know if he said dudes. I'll have to ask grandpa when I get back home. So whatcha wanna do now?"

His four new friends shot him squinty-eyed looks.

"I think," said Jesus, "that Daniel is asking us what we want to do now."

"Yep, that's it, guys," Daniel said.

At that moment, a camel herder drove his half-dozen camels past the boys.

"Wow!" shouted Daniel T. "Those are camels. I've never seen real camels in person. Come on, let's go check 'em out." He turned and ran after the herder and herd. The other boys followed.

Not far off, in the outskirts of the village, was a small oasis. About it grew several palm like trees. The villagers used the oasis to water their stock, which they herded to the water source. Through mutual agreement, each owner of stock animals to be watered had a time during the day to take them to the oasis. Herders who had many animals had two and some times three agreed upon times at the watering hole.

The village had two wells that provided water for the human populace. Besides checking out live camels, Daniel T. Reese was to confront and be confronted by hundreds of strange and mistifying traits, customs, methods, modes, and manners in Nazareth—home to young Jesus Christ.

CHAPTER 5

The five boys hung around the oasis so that Daniel could check out the various animals that the villagers herded there to drink. Sometime after they arrived, Levi reached into the folds of his tunic and pulled out a ball constructed of rawhide tightly wrapped around and around a core of rounded stone. Its diameter was approximately that of a modern-day hard baseball.

He and Joshua tossed it back and forth. Daniel finally took note and said, "Hey, guys, let me see that ball." Joshua tossed it over to him. Daniel caught it one handed, and he turned it around several times. "Wow! This is a cool baseball. You guys have a bat and gloves to go with it?"

None of the boys responded.

"Aw, man, don't tell me. You dudes don't know what I am talking about, huh? OK, let's go sit down in the shade, and I will clue you in."

The four boys followed Daniel T., and they all sat down under one of the nearby olive trees. It took close to half an hour of Daniel talking, gesticulating, and drawing in the dirt, but finally the boys had a grasp of how to play baseball.

Jesus said that he could fashion a bat back at his father's carpentry shop. Levi said that he could talk the leather smith into making gloves if Daniel would draw a likeness. Joshua said that he would get wool from his father to stuff the gloves with. Abraham said that he would get some goat hides from his father to trade to the leather smith to make the gloves.

Daniel said, "You guys are awesome. So in a few days we play ball."

"We can play ball now," said Abraham. "We will teach you how. Since the game is for the same amount of players on each side and we are five, Daniel, you watch until you learn, and then each of us will take turns playing and not playing."

The game that unfolded, to Daniel's eyes, was, in fact, a form of soccer pretty much the same as is know in the modern world: there were two teams and two goals, and no use of hands. The only real difference was the ball: it was small and solid. As the game got going, Daniel caught on quickly and said, "Man, that's gotta be tough on the feet." He glanced at his sandals and figured that he would to have a talk with the sandal maker about making something with a little more protection.

Several days later, not only Jesus, Abraham, Levi, and Joshua but also several other boys from the village of Nazareth engaged in that all-American game we all know as baseball.

Gosh! exclaimed Daniel T. to himself, *I wonder if I can explain hot dogs good enough to have someone make 'em?*

Ten or so minutes after the first baseball game in Nazareth commenced, there were spectators on each side of the playing field. Daniel T., playing pitcher, glanced right and left and took in the growing onlookers. With the thought of hot dogs still in his mind, he said aloud "Could happen!" Then he smiled big and threw his pitch.

Daniel T. had been in Nazareth for five days, and he still believed that he would find his way back to Vancouver, Washington, and his family and friends there. He was beginning to miss them tremendously. He missed the people, television, and video games, as well as his computer, food, and even his pesky little sister.

What I wouldn't do for a Big Mac and fries, Daniel would say to himself a couple of times a day. He thought what he had been eating in the home of Joseph and Mary was OK—a little strange, but it tasted all right: stew with goat meat and vegetables—carrots, lentils, onion—and the seasoning that Mother Mary threw in tasted pretty good. Unleavened bread wasn't bad either, but boy oh boy, thinking of a Big Mac got Daniel T.'s mouth flowing. If he shut his eyes tight, squished up his shoulders, and concentrated really hard, he could smell a Big Mac and French fries.

During the boys' quiet time sitting under an olive tree, Daniel described hamburgers and fries to Jesus, Joshua, Abraham, and Levi. Jesus told him that he thought his mother could make such a thing—the hamburger at least. He was not too sure about the fries. However, the villagers only ate beef on special occasions.

"Say," Daniel said, "where did you guys learn to play soccer? Your foot-and-ball game?"

Levi answered, "The Romans play it. They use a bigger ball, but we think it is more challenging with a smaller one. But they don't call it soccer; they call it football."

"Yeah, right!" Daniel replied with a smirk. "Let me tell you about American football. I think you guys will agree that it is a little different from the Roman's game. First of all, the ball used is just a might different from the one they and you use. It is not round, big, or small, it is…Oh man, how do I explain how our football is shaped? Here, gather around. I'll draw one for you all."

As the boys gathered around Daniel, he grabbed a short stick and drew in the dirt the shape and approximate size of an American football. Then he took the time to explain to the boys the ins and outs of the game.

"But you gotta wear special stuff to play and not get all banged up," Daniel told them. "Another thing about football is that hot dogs and Coke really go good with it."

CHAPTER 6

After supper, Jesus and Daniel took a walk and again found themselves at the oasis. They sat down under a palm tree and Daniel asked Jesus if he planned to follow in his father's footsteps.

Jesus turned to Daniel. "It will depend on where he would be going. I might not want to go there. If he invited me or asked that I go with him, of course I would follow."

"Huh?" uttered a mystified Daniel, looking at Jesus with a slinky eye. "Oh, oh, I get it: follow your father's footsteps! What that means is to do what he does to earn a living. Will you became a carpenter also?"

Nodding his head, Jesus said. "I understand now, and perhaps I will follow in my father's footsteps for a time. How long? I do not know. Maybe I will become a fisherman."

"You know what?" Daniel said. "The more we talk, the more I feel that we met before somehow, somewhere. I get this feeling that I may know more about you than you know about yourself at this time. Tell me about you. Where were you born? Tell me about Mary and Joseph. Why do I feel that I knew them, too, before Joseph brought me here? It's weird but so cool too!"

"Daniel," said Jesus. "I am absolutely certain that we never met prior to my father, Joseph, bringing you to our house. I will tell you about my father, my mother, and me. What I know anyway. I was born in Bethlehem.

"My father and mother went there because of a census. My father had to be there, and while my parents were there, I arrived. Later, when I was one or maybe two years old, we went to Egypt and we were there a short while before returning to Nazareth. Mother and father have been talking about going to Jerusalem for Passover, and they will take us all. You are here now, so you will go also."

"OK," Daniel said. "So what is this Passover? Pass over a bridge to get to the other side?"

"You are close, Dan. Passover is the annual celebration of when Egypt let my people go. They had been held there as slaves. When they left—after 430 years—they came to the Red Sea, and Moses parted the waters so the Israelite's, my people, could Passover and continue on to our land. Passover is celebrated from the fifteenth to the twenty-second of Nisan (April) in Jerusalem. Will you go with us, Daniel?"

"Jerusalem, eh? So that is maybe why people from there are known as Jews? I think I have heard that word at one time or another, Jesus," Daniel said.

"It very well might come to that, Dan. I do know that my people did come from a place that is known as Judea. There are Romans there."

"You know what, Jesus? I do think we have met somewhere before. Every day that goes by, something is said that I think is poking at stuff in my head. Weird, huh?"

Jesus looked at Daniel sideways and said, "Dan, what exactly does that word mean?"

"Huh?" Daniel grunted. "Which word you talking about, man? I must have yelped out fifteen or twenty."

"Weird, Daniel. Weird! What does it mean, man?" Jesus said with a serious questing look all over his twelve-year-old face.

"Far out, Jesus! You said man just like you have always used it as you did, dude. You be da man!" Daniel cried out and smacked Jesus on one shoulder.

Jesus, with a smile on his lips, said, "Far out, dude! You are able to tell that I am not a girl."

Daniel, with an astonished and pleased look stamped across his face, replied "Are you certain that you have not been someplace other than here, Jesus? Like where I am from?"

Jesus placed an arm across Daniel's shoulders. "Where are you from, Daniel?" he asked.

"Beats me," Daniel replied.

"I do not think that will be necessary, Dan. One day you will recall all."

"You think?" Daniel said. "Do you really, really think so?"

"We shall see, dude," said Jesus.

Jesus and Daniel turned to look when they heard voices. Abraham, Joshua, and Levi where headed toward them.

Several days had passed since Daniel's arrival in Nazareth, and now he was apart of the in crowd. Levi carried a sack that contained balls, gloves, and the bat Jesus, with Daniel's help, had fashioned in his father's carpentry shop.

They poured everything out of the sack, and all the boys looked at and handled all of the items. They each tried on the gloves.

"Is it too late to throw a ball around?" Levi asked.

"If we were where I came from, streetlights would come on, and we could play," Daniel told them. Every day, he remembered more of his life back where he lived. He was pretty sure he had known Jesus before he had awakened in Nazareth—maybe the other boys too. If he didn't know them outright, Daniel felt he had heard all their names at sometime, somehow, and somewhere.

"Streetlights?" asked Abe. "Like torches?"

"Yeah, something like that but without fire," Daniel said.

All the boys looked at each other.

Abraham said, "Right!

CHAPTER 7

Boys being boys, they hunkered down and set to shooting the breeze about this and that—girls included.

"You really, really have not ever been on an ass at all?" Joshua asked Daniel.

"Nope, not ever. I've never even been close to one," replied Daniel.

"My father, Joseph, has a load of wood for our carpentry being delivered, and I will ask the drover to allow me to unhitch the ass so that you can mount it, and I will lead you on it for a while."

"You are so, so cool, Jesus," Daniel said enthusiastically.

"So, I am the man, huh?" Jesus, with a bright smile across his youthful countenance, shot back.

"You know, I have a strange feeling that you really are, or that you will be, the man at sometime," said a pensive Daniel T. Reese.

After that, the boys headed to their homes. The homes were adobe brick or tents, but they were adequate. All had wooden outhouses a distance off for sanitation. Each had a hearth of some sort or another for cooking.

Early the following morning, Daniel could not leave his sleeping pallet fast enough. He was all excited and more than ready to mount and ride a donkey.

"No," he corrected himself, "an ass."

Joseph, Jesus, James, and Salome were all gathered around their stone hearth. Mother Mary was ladling a corn and potato mush into bowls. Unleavened bread was awaiting all.

A thought crossed Daniel's mind as he scooted between Joseph and Jesus. *Why does Jesus always say, "My father, Joseph" whenever he is talking about him? Is there another father? We all know who his father is. Or do we?*

Again, Daniel had that strange feeling that he had met his wonderful new friends before, or knew more about them than he could recall. *But how, when, where, or why?*

Shortly thereafter, a raucousness sounded from outside.

Little Salome jumped and shouted, "He is here, Daniel. You will get to go on your first ass ride—if he will let you."

Daniel shot a slinky-eyed look at Jesus and said, "You told her? Why?"

"It is not a crime to not have been on an ass before, Dan. After all,"

Jesus said, "you may not have any where you are from. How do you get from one far away place to another?"

"Hmm. I'll tell you sometime," said Daniel.

"How about you two strong boys go outside with me to off-load our wood? Then we will talk to Ishmael about unhitching his ass so Daniel can ride it," said Joseph.

"I want to see that," said Salome and James in unison.

Ishmael's ass was unhitched and a rope was fastened around its nose with a short length on either side of the knot just below the lower jaw to be used as reins.

Joseph helped Daniel mount the ass, and then Jesus handed Daniel the rope reins and said, "You pull on the rope on the side that leads in the direction you want him to go. To get him moving forward, you loosen up on the ropes and you kick him softly on both sides and go *tech, tech, tech.*"

"Got it," said Daniel as he got the ass moving. "Hey!" he yelled from the short distance his ass had gone. "How do I stop him?"

"Pull back on the reins," Jesus said.

"I think I like cars better," Daniel said as he was helped to dismount after his short ride.

"What are cars?" asked Jesus.

"Tell you later!" Daniel said.

"Why do you not speak more about where you came from and your people there?" asked Jesus.

"Well," said Daniel, "since I woke up in the street here in Nazareth and since I don't know how I got here, I also don't know very much about where I came from and the people there!"

"You do not know of your mother and father, brothers and sisters?" asked Jesus.

"No, I don't, but maybe someday I will remember. Some things seem to creep into my mind now and then, but only parts of stuff—like cars. I seem to know that word—cars—and that I may like them better than Ismael's ass, but I don't really know what they are or what they look like or what they do.

"I really want to remember my family, Jesus, and I want to find them someday. I hope it happens soon, because being around you and your family makes me miss them terribly."

"We will be going to Jerusalem soon, Dan. Maybe you will find them there or get word of who they are or where they may be," Jesus said.

CHAPTER 8

Days came and went. Daniel helped Jesus and Joseph in the carpentry shop doing whatever was asked of him. While he took a handsaw and cut a section of plank and then took a hand-operated drill to bore as he had been shown, his mind kicked in.

He asked himself, w*hy do I remember power tools, baseball, and football, as well as some of the words we use where I came from and that I came from Vancouver? Weird, man! Like I remember cars and that they were better than donkeys, but better how? And why would I think that?*

Although all those thoughts crossed his mind, Daniel kept at his assigned tasks and completed them in a timely manner and to the best of his ability.

Jesus tapped Daniel on the shoulder and said, "Dan, let us go sit outside for a while. We have been working without a break in our labors for long enough."

Daniel turned to him and with a very pleased smile replied, "Cool, dude. Let's do it."

Outside, they found some shade and sat down with their backs to one of the walls of Joseph's carpentry shop.

"The day is coming up soon," said Jesus.

"What day are you talking about?" asked Daniel.

"The day that we leave to travel to Jerusalem," Jesus said. "You are going with us, Daniel, are you not?"

"Yes, of course I am! What would I do here by myself?" replied Daniel. "And just how far is it to Jerusalem, and how do we get there?"

"It is not so far—only five days away, Dan," Jesus said.

"Jesus, Jesus! Five days? And how will we get there?" asked an astounded young Daniel.

Jesus looked at Daniel and asked him, "Dan, why did you say my name twice? I am sitting right next to you."

"Did I do that?" Daniel replied. "I don't know why I did that, but anyway, five days? Why does it take so long? How far is Jerusalem anyway?"

"Well, Daniel, as I said," Jesus continued, "it is five days away."

"Why does it take five days? Won't we be riding asses or maybe camels?" asked a miffed young Daniel.

"No, Dan. Only women and girls and very young boys ride asses," Jesus said.

"How about camels, than Jesus?"

"No, Dan. Camels are hard to ride, and they do not like it at all," replied Jesus. "They are used for pack animals. They will carry our food and bedrolls along with the animals' feed."

"Are there any towns along the way? If not, then I take it that we will be eating and sleeping under the stars," Daniel said, "and cooking over an open fire. Pretty much like at home, huh?"

"There will be a lot of people from Nazareth going also. Everyone here, except ones too old or too young and those who are needed to care for them, will be on the road," Jesus said. "Also, Dan, along the way will be people from all around the city. We will have a lot of company at campfires. It will not be a lonely trip."

"OK," said Daniel. "How about in Jerusalem? Will we all camp out in the streets there?"

"No, Daniel. During Passover, free room and food for us all and the animals is provided by the homeowners there," Jesus said.

"Huh!" exclaimed Daniel. "Five days on foot. How far are we to walk each day and just how far is Nazareth from Jerusalem?"

"All I can tell you, all I know is that Jerusalem is five days away from Nazareth, Dan. Of course, that is only day travel. If one traveled into the night," Jesus said with a shrug, "maybe it would not be that many days."

"So," said Daniel, "you said a lot of other people from here will be going too. Then Abraham, Joshua, and Levi will be coming along?"

"Yes, they will," said Jesus. "When we all stop along the way for supper, we will get together with them and go see others at their campfires and talk about this and that—baseball maybe."

"When will we be leaving?" Daniel asked.

"Well," said Jesus, "tomorrow we start preparing for the trip. It will take two days to get everything ready. Then early on the third day, we will load up the camels. We will take two camels and two asses. The camels will carry all the food, bedrolls, hay, and oats, and mother and Salome will ride the asses, which will also carry the water bags. Then when we get to Jerusalem, it will be two days before Passover celebration begins, and we will use that time to care for the animals and to get acquainted with our hosts."

They started early the following day helping gather all that was needed for the trips to and from Jerusalem. Two days quickly slipped by. On the third day, the camels were fully loaded. The women mounted the asses and were ready to travel. Joseph led one camel with the second tethered behind him, and Jesus and Daniel walked alongside the two asses carrying Mary and Salome.

CHAPTER 9

As they trudged along the route to Jerusalem, Daniel was all eyes. He, being from the Pacific Northwest, had never seen anything like what was passing before his eyes during their journey. It was not that the terrain was bleak or desolate; it was just different, but Daniel could not know or remember how or why he thought that.

Jesus's brother, James, maintained the lead ahead of his mother and his sister as he led the two camels along. His father kept a watchful eye on him but let him take over the camel lead rope. James, at nine years of age, felt extremely proud.

Turning to his father, who walked alongside him, James said, "Father, have you noticed how quiet Daniel has been and how he keeps looking about as if he is searching for something? Maybe he is remembering where he came from."

Joseph smiled at his young son and said, "That would be a very good thing for him, James. Then we could help him return to his people."

Approximately two hours before the sun set, the caravan began to pull off the road, and they set about putting together campsites—each to their own liking. After setting up camp, caring for the animals, and enjoying their evening meal after the first day's march, all that anyone seemed to want to do was lay back and recuperate. Even the boys were quiet. Most were in their bedrolls.

Daniel had said good night, and then he lay upon his bedroll and looked up at the stars.

"Were there that many stars at night where I came from?" he quietly asked himself. "Somehow, I don't think so. Why I wonder. Why not? Aren't they the same stars as here? Why wouldn't they be? And what about what is out there, or should I say what is not? There is not much of anything other than rocks, sand, bushes, and gardens or farms here and there. I seem to remember—oh, I don't know what, but something.

Shortly, Daniel fell asleep.

The next morning, everyone gathered around the cooking fire that Joseph had set ablaze. Mary and Salome were busy heating the leftovers that they had cooked the night before. Up and down the campsite, all the travelers seemed to be doing likewise.

After the morning meal, all the men and older boys loaded up their pack animals. Then the women mounted the asses and the caravan headed out.

As they got under way, Jesus edged closer to Daniel and got his attention. "Daniel, you have not spoken more than a dozen words this morning. Is something troubling you?"

Daniel glanced at Jesus as they trudged on and replied, "No, nothing's troubling me, man. Something has been going in my mind off and on, like I begin to remember something about this and that about where I came from, but I cannot get much of anything, and then it is gone. Why do I know my name and know some things like power tools, baseball, and stuff?"

"Maybe because those are things you cared about greatly," Jesus told him.

"That might be, but surely I cared about many things, Jesus. Surely, I loved my father and mother. Why don't I remember them? Their faces? Their names? What about sisters and brothers? I may have them too."

Jesus moved closer to Daniel as they walked along. He reached over and gently placed his hand on Daniel's left shoulder. "Someday, Daniel, all will come back to you."

Immediately, Daniel felt his soul lift and his body relax. He looked at Jesus with gratitude bursting out of him.

"For real, Jesus."

As the noon sun was high in the sky, the caravan halted for a short while to partake of leavened bread and dried dates, and to feed and water the animals, which included some dogs.

Soon the camels where repacked and ready to be led once again down the road to the next stop. There the caravan would halt and make ready for their second overnight stop.

During their supper, Joseph asked, "Daniel, how many times have you been to Jerusalem, and how long since the last time you were there?"

"I have not ever been to Jerusalem, sir," Daniel said.

"Not ever?" Joseph asked.

"No, sir," Daniel replied. "Not ever, sir."

"What is this 'sir' you keep saying?" Joseph asked.

Daniel, dumbfounded at first, didn't know how to answer. Then he said, "I think that where I came from that was what we called big people when we talked with them. I think. With men, you see? I think with women there may be another word. Um—but I don't remember what that might be."

"I think I understand," said Joseph, "So I am a sir, huh?"

"Yes, sir," said Daniel with a large smile. "Yes, sir. For sure."

During the journey, Daniel gazed at the countryside and spotted animals as they came by and momentarily stopped to watch the caravan pass. He knew not what they were, but he had seen antelope, badgers, vultures, wolves, and, maybe, a couple of coyotes.

In the evenings after super, the boys, Jesus, Daniel, Abraham, Joshua, Levi, and some of the other boys from family's camped nearby, got together to shoot the breeze. Mainly, Daniel listened as the main topic was about Passover celebrations and what they had done in Jeruselum before, what they would do during the current visit, and what they wanted to see.

Jesus had said little about anything. He leaned toward Daniel and whispered, "As you, Daniel, I prefer to listen."

CHAPTER 10

A short time after the sun was halfway to nightfall, the caravan arrived in the city of Jerusalem. As during past arrivals, homeowners were there to greet the travelers. Couples with no children and those with one or two soon were offered accommodations for themselves and their animals. Those with three or more children were picked later, but none were left without shelter—that included the single men and women.

Not long after the Nazarene's were sheltered and cared for, people came to Jerusalem for Passover from many directions, and they were all taken care of by homeowners who provided shelter and food at no cost for all, including the animals. Although Daniel could not remember his life in Vancouver, he hoped it was a place comparable to Jerusalem.

"How long does Passover last?" Daniel asked Jesus.

"Seven days," Jesus told him. "You will have plenty of time to familiarize yourself with the city. I will help you. I have some special things that I want to do."

The following day, Daniel was anxious to see Jerusalem. Joseph told Daniel and Jesus that they were free to go after the animals were fed. Their host, Emanuel, showed them where the feed was kept. Joseph had told him that the boys were capable and knew what to do.

Jesus and Daniel jumped to it and fed the animals in record time. Afterward, Jesus and Daniel rounded up Abraham, Joshua, and Levi, who had also finished with their assigned chores and had permission to go out.

"What are we going to do?" the boys asked Jesus.

"We will take Daniel around the city and let him see all there is to see," Jesus said.

"Yeah! That would be cool, dudes. Let's get 'er done," exclaimed Daniel joyously.

As they led him around, Daniel asked about this and that as he took in the city. When they neared the marketplace, Daniel spied three ladies nearby. He elbowed Jesus and asked, "Who are those women over there?" He pointed them out. "The ones in the fancy robes and all the jewelry."

Jesus looked and took them into view. "They are sinners, Dan," he told him.

"Why are they sinners, Jesus? Did they steal all the stuff they are wearing? The robes and jewels?"

"No, Daniel. The robes and jewels belong to them."

"Then why are they sinners?" Daniel asked.

By then the other boys where all listening, and they looked over at Jesus with questioning eyes.

"They are sinners because they dress to draw men to them. They then entertain them as if they were married," Jesus said.

"The men they entertain, are they sinners too?" Daniel asked.

Jesus looked at all the boys. "Yes, they are," he said.

As their show and tell progressed, Daniel was totally enthralled. He felt that Jerusalem was definitely beautiful. A thought crossed his twelve-year-old mind and he blurted it out. "Hey, the general countryside outside of the city looks kind of dry. Where or how does the city get water for the people and the animals?"

"I know. I know," Levi exclaimed.

They all turned to Levi and he said, "I once heard my father talking with some friends about just that: water for Jerusalem. There are the Solomon Pools with aqueducts to the city and also what is called Gihon Spring. And some people have pools and cisterns to catch and store rain."

"Yes," said Joshua, "very much like we have in Nazareth."

As the day went by, Daniel was enthralled with all he saw. He wondered if where he came from was as lovely as Jerusalem. As hard as he tried, Daniel could not visualize or remember how and why he had woken up in Nazareth. So how could he expect to know what where he came from looked like? He shook his head to clear it of such contemplation as the five boys came to a stop at a large and elaborate building.

"Boy!" Daniel said. "What is that?"

Jesus said, "That is the Temple."

"OK. But what is it called?" Daniel asked. "What is its name"

Jesus and the other boys looked at Daniel. "The Temple," Jesus said.

"Can we go in and look?" Daniel asked.

"Not now," said Jesus. "Maybe later."

The boys continued showing Daniel Jerusalem. As supper approached, the boys were well on their way to their hosts' homes and arrived early enough to feed the asses and camels. That was their only daily chore every morning and every night. The boys didn't balk since it was also their duty back at home in Nazareth.

The days of Passover soon passed. The Nazarenes and the other people who had come to Jerusalem from everywhere for the celebration were saying good-bye and thanking their hosts before getting under way for their journeys home.

Jesus got Daniel's attention and signaled him to follow as he walked away from the caravan and his family.

"What are we doing?" asked Daniel. "Why are we walking away?"

Jesus did not respond and moved on quickly.

"Hey, man. Yo, dude!" Daniel yelled after him. "What are we doing? Aren't we going with your family?"

"No, I am not," Jesus said. "You can turn around and go with them, Daniel."

Daniel caught up with Jesus and said, "No, I am going with you. I don't know what you have in your mind to do, but it must be pretty important to get you to abandon your family. They will wonder where you are and worry. Maybe they will wonder about me also."

"They will think that we are just lagging behind, Daniel."

"Are we just lagging behind, Jesus?" Daniel asked, his face dripping with consternation. "How soon will we turn back to join them, dude? And why are we doing this anyway?"

Jesus did not respond and just walked on. Daniel followed and asked no more questions.

They located what appeared to be a city park. It was in fact where people who came and went from outside of the city could tether their animals until they were ready to depart, either the same day or soon after.

"We will spend the night here when we are ready," Jesus said to Daniel.

Daniel looked at him quizzically and then asked, "When did you come up with this escapade, Jesus?"

"Remember when you asked about the Temple? That is when I knew that I needed to be in there, Dan."

"Why?" Daniel asked. "What is in there that you have to see?"

"Not see, Dan, listen to and speak with."

"Today? Right now?"

"Maybe not today, but surely tomorrow," Jesus said.

"Your father and mother will miss you—us. Won't they come looking for us?"

"Maybe after a time," Jesus told him. "You saw how many people make up the caravan. They may not accept that we are missing right away."

CHAPTER 11

Jesus led Daniel thru the market to one of the fruit stands. "You like dates, Dan?" he asked.

"Sure I do. Fresh or dried."

"Good," Jesus said. "Come and pick your choice or some of each."

"Yeah, sure! And how are we to pay?" Daniel asked with a slinky-eye shot at Jesus.

"I have coins—shekels, talents, and some drachmas—Dan."

"I take it that those are the coins of the realm. Don't you have paper money?"

"What is paper money?" Jesus queried.

"Oh man! You know, money made from paper, dude."

"Daniel, tell me what money is and tell me what paper is that money is made of."

"Um, I don't know any of that, Jesus. I really don't know where that all came from or why. I don't know what paper and money are."

Jesus looked over at Daniel and slowly shook his head then smiled. "Do you want some dates or other fruit? I really do have some coins."

"And just where did you get coins, Jesus? You didn't steal them, did you?"

"No, Dan. They were given to me by my father's customers when I took them the orders he made for them."

"Cool, man! I do love those dried dates," warbled Daniel. "I never had them before I came here—um, how would I know that? Maybe I did, huh, Jesus? Well, I sure liked them when I had them back at your house and on the road to Jerusalem."

They had a handful each and then got some pastries from another vendor before leaving the market.

After an extended walkabout, they ended up back in the park and located a place to settle down.

Daniel said, "Hey, buddy, I take it that we will be spending the night here. If so, how about bedrolls, huh? How about—never mind! This here is your show. You just gotta get in that temple, huh? OK than!"

"Daniel, we will break off some shrubs and bring them back here to lie upon. It will be fun," Jesus said with glee.

"Right!" Daniel shot back. "Hey, what is your middle name?"

"Middle name? Why would anyone need such?"

"I really don't know," Daniel replied. "But I guess there is a reason."

"You told us that your name is Daniel T. Reese. Why the 'T?' What does it mean?"

"I don't remember, Jesus. What is your family name?"

"Ah!" Jesus said. "Mary, Jesus, James, and Salome of Joseph from Nazareth."

"OK, dude. I get that. You know what? Let's go find some shrubs to tear up and drag back here for our beds. I will be ready to lie down by then."

Early the following morning, just shortly after the sun appeared on the far horizon, Jesus reached over and shook Daniel awake.

"Let's go to the market, Dan. I am hungry. Let's go there and get hot, fresh pastries and dates."

Daniel sat up, rubbed his face with both hands, and said to Jesus, "Food! Yes, man! I think I can wolf down some of that."

"Let us go then, but we will gather up our shrubs and pile them up in those bushes over there. They will be there for us tonight," said Jesus.

It did not take long for the two twelve-year-old boys to get 'er done and be on their way.

"Did you slumber well, Dan?" Jesus asked as they walked.

"Yes. Yes, I did, but I had strange dreams. I dreamed that I was somewhere—I don't know where—and I was with some boys. I don't think I ever saw their faces. If I did, I don't remember what they looked like. We were doing something, but I don't remember what."

"You know what else? I do remember this. You were there, too. You stood off to the side, alone, and never moved or said a word. The sun was behind you, and it made you look like you had a ring of stickers on your head. Weird, huh?"

Jesus shook his head and slid a sideways quizzical look at the strange boy who walked beside him.

"I hope you have a lot of coins," Daniel said. "I'm really hungry."

They arrived at the market, and soon their hands were full of pastries and dates.

They found a spot to hunker down and enjoy their meal.

As they ate, Daniel looked around. He turned to Jesus and said, "Remember when I brought up paper money? I told you that I don't know what paper or money are."

"Yes, I remember," Jesus said. "Do you now know?"

"No, I don't really. You see that man over there in the blue robe, the one who is holding something in his hands?"

Jesus looked where Daniel pointed.

"Yes, I see," he said.

"Do you know what he is holding?" Daniel asked.

"Yes, he has in his hands a section of parchment."

"Parchment? What is that?" asked Daniel.

"Well," replied Jesus, "parchment is made of several things. It can be made from plants such as reeds and from animal hides. I suppose many more things can be made into parchment."

"OK. And what is parchment used for, Jesus?"

"For one thing, Dan. To keep a tally."

"What is that, this tally thing?"

"A tally is a count: how many or how much there is of what you want to keep track of. Look, Dan," Jesus then took his right hand and pointed to each finger of his left hand, "the tally of fingers on my left hand is five."

"And then what, Jesus? What do they do with the tally?"

"It is marked on the parchment."

"I think I remember something—but what?" Daniel said.

"Daniel," Jesus said as they sat and munched their food, "you asked about names in the middle, which I take to mean between two other names. Why anyone would need three is beyond me. You have three, Dan. Do you know why? And what does 'T' mean? Is that a name? 'T?'"

Daniel looked hard at Jesus and suddenly he knew. His eyes opened wide, his mouth stretched across his face, and he jumped up.

"I know now! Just this very minute. 'T' is for Thomas. Jesus, that is my middle name!"

"Fine," Jesus said, "but do you now also know why you need three names, Daniel Thomas Reese?"

"Naw, man, I don't. There must be a reason, dude," said Daniel. "Hey, Jesus," Daniel began, changing the subject. "What do you want to do now? Let's go check out the sinner ladies and see what color they have on today. Ya know, dude, they might be sinners, but they are sure lookers, huh?"

Daniel, at twelve, was at the beginning of hormone rage. He didn't know what was going on, but the draw of the opposite sex was there.

Jesus only smiled and said, "No, Dan, I am going to the Temple. You can wait outside and people watch."

"I don't think so, man! I'm going in with you to check it out and see if I can determine why it is a big draw for you," Daniel squeaked out. "Say, Jesus, on the way there, we might pass the sinner ladies, huh?"

CHAPTER 12

Jesus reached inside his tunic and withdrew some coins. He gave them to Daniel and said, "You stay away from the sinners. Take these shekels. If you see something you want, buy it. Daniel, I am referring to food."

"Yes, oh master! Nothing else but. Thank you."

As he turned and waved to Jesus, Daniel thought, *Hmm! Now exactly what else do I want to buy?*

Jesus climbed the steps and went into the Temple.

After about two hours worth of trumping through the market, Daniel had eaten his fill of dried dates and goat cheese. He then came upon an ancient bearded man sitting on an up-turned crate of some sort. A small friendly dog lay at the man's feet.

Daniel asked the obvious owner if he could pet the dog and was given the go ahead. As he did so, Daniel's thoughts turned inward, and he began to visualize another dog, but the vision evaporate very quickly.

What was that? Daniel asked himself. *Do I have a dog back where I came from? Why can I not remember? How and why am I here? If I have a family, do they know where I am now? If they don't know, are they worried and searching for me? And Jesus, are Joseph, Mary, James, and Salome worried because we are not with them?*

After leaving the man and the dog, Daniel found himself at the Temple. He hesitated momentarily and then climbed the steps to the portals. After wandering through the building, Daniel soon located Jesus and went over to where he was standing.

"Hey, dude. What's doing?" he asked. "Whatever they are talking about, you look like you are into it. Do you really understand what is being said? You are only twelve years old just like me. What I have heard so far is way over my head."

Jesus looked at his companion. "Yes, I do understand what is being said. Whether it is right or wrong, good or bad is another thing."

Daniel just looked at Jesus and thought, *I don't know how or why, but I have a strong feeling that he will tell them a thing or two about what is what and how it should be.*

The kids remained in the Temple during the entire time that the doctors and teachers took turns speaking.

Daniel didn't speak another word. He kept his attention on what was being discussed, and he kept a close eye on Jesus, who was also silent. It was quite evident that he, too, was focused on what was being said.

Finally, the meeting was over for that day. As Daniel and Jesus exited the Temple, just beyond the portals, Daniel tugged on Jesus's sleeve and brought him to a stop.

"How could you possibly understand what was being discussed in there? Those guys all talked like they know a lot of stuff that you and I are way too young to know."

"I don't know how or why, but I did understand them," Jesus said.

It was now approaching the night of their second day alone in Jerusalem. Jesus and Daniel were sprawled out on their shrubs, looking up at the moon and stars that were starting to fill the sky.

"Hey, Jesus, what do you want to do tomorrow? After we eat, of course?" Daniel asked. "You do still have some coins, right? Oh, please, please tell me you do, 'cause I just know that I am gonna be starving by morning. Say, what are we going to do if you don't have shekels and talents, and those other ones—drama something. How will we live? What kind of work could we do to get coins?"

"We will think of something, Daniel," Jesus said.

"Yeah, sure!" Daniel threw back at him. "Like get a paper route or shine shoes, huh?"

"What? What is it you are saying?" Jesus asked.

Daniel, with an absolutely astonished look on his face, shrugged with both shoulders and stuttered, "I-I-I d-don't know where that came fr-from, Jesus. I know I said it, but I don't know what it means. What was it I said?"

"I don't know, Daniel. I was looking at the moon and stars, and I did not hear what you said then."

"Well, let us forget it. Since I don't know what I said, then it is no big loss, Jesus."

Jesus smiled up at the sky.

"How long are we going to stay in Jerusalem? We will go back to Nazareth sometime, right?" Daniel asked.

"Yes. I am certain that we will," said Jesus. "Soon."

The morning of their third day alone in Jerusalem, Daniel said, "Jesus—"

Before he got another word out, Jesus said, "Yes. Yes, Daniel, we will go to the marketplace right away. You don't have to say it. I know you are hungry."

"Yes, I am, but that is not what I was going to say. I was going to point out to you that our shrubs have dried and by tonight they will not be any good as beds. I say we should dump them and go get more now so that we will have them for tonight," Daniel exclaimed.

"You know, Daniel, you are a smart—um, how do you say? Oh yes, you are a smart dude," Jesus said with a twinkle in his eye and a wide grin on his face.

After disposing the old shrubs, gathering fresh replacements, and concealing them, the boys made their way to the market and chowed down.

Daniel asked, "What shall we do now? How about we slide by and check out the sinners, you know, just to admire their robes and their jewels."

"You may do whatever you want, Daniel. I am going to the Temple."

"Why?" asked a mystified Daniel. "Did you not get enough of listening to those stuffy old dudes? Wouldn't you rather go and look at pretty ladies in pretty robes and a lot of jewels?"

"No, Daniel. Today, I will not only listen but also speak."

"About what, man? Did you really understand what they were saying yesterday? What are you gonna talk to them about?"

"This, that, and the other," Jesus said with a couple of nods.

Daniel silently followed Jesus to the Temple. Inside, discussions among the elders there were in full swing. Jesus and Daniel took a stance off to the side and listened as first one distinguished individual spoke to the group and then another followed.

During a lull, Jesus stepped in and began speaking to the group. He had quietly listened to the speakers in turn and now he meant to speak his mind.

Daniel, in utter amazement, stood by and gazed at his twelve-year-old companion. Jesus spoke for quite some time. While he spoke, Joseph and Mary entered the Temple. As they approached, Jesus, Daniel, and the doctors and teachers who were listening to Jesus turned away and began their lectures once again.

Joseph stepped to Jesus and gently tugged on him, gesturing for him to come along. Mary placed an arm across Jesus's shoulders and motioned for Daniel to follow.

Outside beyond the Temple, Mary turned to Jesus and asked. "Son, how could you do this to us? Your father and I and many others in our caravan looked everywhere for you. After the first day, we arranged for Levi's parents to take James and Salome with them. We brought one camel and one ass back to Jeruselum with us. We arrived last night. Our hosts for Passover agreed to shelter the animals and us while we searched for you. We are thankful that you both are safe."

"I am truly sorry to have caused you worry and anguish," Jesus said.

CHAPTER 13

During the five-day trek back to Nazareth, not much was said until the travelers sat around their cooking fire and finished their evening meal. The first night, Mary asked Jesus what he had been saying to the elders in the Temple.

"I was pointing out to them how we should treat each other and be treated—all of us all the time. We should help one another as needed. Love thy brother—forgive any trespasses upon thee," Jesus said.

Mary gazed at her beloved son with unquenchable love and emotion. Joseph stood and embraced Jesus. His heart was bursting with pride.

Daniel had been silent and took in all that was said.

He is twelve, as I am. How did he learn what he said? Daniel asked himself.

On the evening of the fifth day, they arrived in Nazareth. Mary walked to Levi's parents' household to retrieve her children. James and Salome ran to her, and they nearly topple her over as they hugged their mother.

The following morning, life commenced as if the Jerusalem trip had not taken place. Jesus and Daniel took to helping Joseph in his carpentry shop as needed. Joseph welcomed their assistance, but he made sure that the boys had plenty of time to be boys.

Jesus and Daniel grabbed every opportunity to get together with Abraham, Joshua, and Levi. Several other boys joined in, and together they worked on perfecting their baseball game.

Soon after they began playing, they drew spectators: men, women, and children. They played until it was suppertime and then gathered up all the equipment in a sack, and Levi carried it home.

After their evening meal, Jesus and Daniel sat outside, leaning against the wall of their home.

Daniel turned to Jesus and asked, "How did you come up with all the stuff you were spouting off to those old dudes in the Temple? Don't get me wrong, man, it sounded righteous, but I don't know if they bought it. It looked like they were getting set to throw us out. You think they believed you?"

"Someday, I will return to the Temple and speak again when I am older so that they will listen to what I say and pay heed," said Jesus.

"Yeah? When do you think that will be?"

"Um? Maybe when I am thirty," Jesus said.

"And, dude, just where did you get all that stuff you were throwing out there?" Daniel asked.

"I'm not certain," Jesus replied. "It was just all there for me to speak it out."

"All right then! What are we gonna do tomorrow? Your father, Joseph, said we would not be needed in the shop."

"Daniel, why did you say 'my father' and then 'Joseph?'" Jesus asked.

"I really don't know, Jesus. I suppose because you do it all the time."

The following day, after the morning meal, Daniel took Jesus aside. "Hey, man, how about we go for a walkabout?"

"A walkabout? A walkabout what?" Jesus asked.

"Not a walkabout anything, Jesus. Man, I don't even know where that came from. I mean let's go out into the countryside and just look around. Other than all of us hiking off to Jerusalem, I haven't been out of Nazareth. I want to see what is out there."

Jesus and Daniel left the confines of the town and walked into the surrounding countryside. Nazareth at that time had a population of four hundred or so. It did not take long before the two twelve-year-old explorers were up in the surrounding low hills and the small trees and shrubbery that grew sparingly there.

As they went farther away from town, the boys began to come across such animals as antelope, foxes, and other small furry creatures. All stood still as Jesus and Daniel went by, and they didn't seem to be frightened.

As Jesus and Daniel crested the next hill and pushed into low shrubs and trees, they heard low menacing growls. Then in front of them appeared a pack of six to eight wolves.

Daniel was startled and frightened. If Jesus had not reached over and held him back, he would have turned and run off.

Jesus said, "No, Daniel, stay. They will not harm us. Come."

He led them to the wolves, which stood motionless until Jesus began petting them. They then rubbed against him and left reluctantly.

Daniel was totally mesmerized and immobile. Jesus reached over to him, placed his palm on Daniel's head, and said, "They are beautiful creatures, are they not? No need to be frightened." Jesus then ruffled Daniel's hair.

By the noon meal, the two boys were safe and sound back in Nazareth.

"How did you do that with the wolves?" Daniel asked of his magical friend.

***

That afternoon, Jesus and Daniel rounded up Abraham, Joshua, Levi, and assorted other friends—all who could come out and play. They had enough boys to form two teams. Baseball had caught on in Nazareth.

The next day, Joseph had enough work to keep Jesus and Daniel busy until noon, and then they were free to go.

After working, they again sat against the house wall in the shade.

Daniel said, "Any little thing you wanna do—that is, that we can do?"

"No, Daniel. I have nothing in mind," Jesus told him.

"Too bad there isn't a river, a lake, or even a stream or a creek so we could go fishing. You ever been fishing, dude?"

"No, I have not, Daniel."

"Someday you should, man. It's fun, and, of course, grilled fish is good eating. Say, you said that when you are older you will return to the Temple. If they listen to you, then you will become a fisher—a fisher of men."

CHAPTER 14

Jesus was busy delivering finished products to customers of the carpenter shop. Daniel was not needed, so he went in search of company. He had located Abraham and Joshua, and now they were sitting at the nearby watering hole. He had been told previously that the watering hole was filled as needed by an aqueduct.

Taking in what was going on there—camels and sheep quenching their thirst—Daniel asked his companions, "Why is it that camels are not ridden and used mainly to carry stuff?"

Joshua told him, "They are very hard to sit on. Their gait is bumpy, and it makes it uncomfortable to sit astride the animal."

Daniel digested that with a headshake and then said, "Hey, you guys, what do you think of our buddy Jesus?"

Many days ago, Daniel had explained the word "buddy" to them.

"What about him?" asked Abraham.

"Doesn't he seem to know a lot of stuff? Where did he learn all of it? You should have heard him in the Temple! Sure, maybe those old dudes weren't really paying attention to what he was saying, but it sounded righteous to me. Man! Like he is only twelve, you know? Where does he get all that stuff?" said Daniel.

Abraham looked over at Joshua. Joshua shrugged his shoulders, shook his head, and said, "I understand what you are saying. Yes, Jesus seems to be somewhat different, but I would not want to stop being his friend."

"What do you think?" Joshua turned and put the question to Abraham.

Abraham was a few months older than Joshua and Jesus, maybe older than Daniel also. He looked off in the distance and then slowly turned to Joshua and Daniel. "Yes. Yes, surely, Jesus is different. I have a very strong feeling that he wants to be a teacher—perhaps to teach us all how to live and let live, and to not harm one another in anyway."

"Hey, hey, guys, that is exactly what he was spouting off to the old dudes in the Temple. And you know what?" Daniel continued. "He told them that later the Temple would come to be known by a different name. A place where people would go to worship God. You know, I may not be able to remember much about where I came from, but I remember God and who he is. He is the father of us all! You know what else? You guys have heard Jesus when refers to his father and he always says 'My father, Joseph!"

"Yeah, yeah," both Abraham and Joshua said in unison.

"So," Abraham said, "he is counting both. His father here on Earth and his father up in heaven."

"Yes," Joshua said. "He is the father of us all."

Daniel spoke up then. "Father to us all, huh? Animals too?"

Joshua and Abraham both said yes with their heads.

"OK," Daneil blurted out. "Why the heck do you suppose he made camels that spit at you and make a loud terrible bleat sound?"

Abraham said, "Maybe so that we humans, in the dark of night, would know that it was a camel we heard. Just like we know a sheep, an ass, a wolf, or any other animal when not seen from the sound it makes with its mouth."

Daniel and Joshua looked at each other. Daniel shot a slinky eye at Abraham and said, "Abe, you've been hanging out with Jesus way too much. You are starting to sound like him. Now, let me tell you what has been up with me the last couple of days. You know I don't remember much about where I'm from, and I don't remember anything about my family: father, mother, brothers, and sisters. During the past nights—two or three—I have had thoughts about what might have been my life before I came here. Not anything solid, just fading images and shadows. One time it was a lot of things moving down what I thought could be a trail. All separate things—some moving one way and others the other way.

"Then one time I was looking up at the sky because there was a loud strange sound up there. The shadow I saw made me think of a big, big bird because it looked like it had wings. What kind of bird could be that big and make very loud strange sounds? Then another time—I guess all of this was in dreams, because I don't think I was awake—I was in something that was moving. I guess it was going someplace and taking me with it. I was sitting inside of whatever it was, and in front of me, there were shapes of people who were also sitting there as we were being taken to I don't know where. I woke up before we got there."

Abraham and Joshua both looked skeptical and were tight jawed—unable to speak readily.

Finally, Joshua spoke up. "A big, big bird making loud strange sounds? And another thing with people in it? Daniel, it had to have been a dream—or dreams. If I were you, I really would watch what I eat, and how much, at night."

Abraham chimed in with a toothy smile and a couple of affirmative headshakes.

After the evening meal, Jesus and Daniel went out and again reclined against a wall. They sat quietly, savoring a lovely serene evening.

After a short while, James and Salome joined them against the wall.

Daniel was the first to break the silence. He said, "Jesus, you told me that you will return to Jerusalem to speak with the, um, elders. That is what they are, right?"

"Yes, Daniel, that is right. They are certainly elders."

"So you will return to Jerusalem for Passover but will stay out of the Temple till you are thirty?" said Daniel.

"I said that, Daniel, yes," Jesus agreed and nodded.

"Do you think they will listen to you then?"

"One can only hope," Jesus said. "If they truly want happy and fulfilled lives, they must learn to accept one another as they are and to extend help to those in need."

Daniel was silent. James and Salome had not yet spoken.

Daniel turned to Jesus and asked, "Are you sure you're twelve?"

All remained silent for a time and then Daniel blurted out, "So besides being a carpenter, what will you be till you are thirty?"

"I will continue to learn, and I will go on walkabouts and pass on to all who will listen how we can please and be closer to God. Walkabouts. Is that correct, Daniel?"

"Yes, just so, Jesus. Just so. God? Who is he, Jesus? I seem to know him—about him—but like all else in my life before I woke up here in Nazareth, I just don't remember. Sure, I remember somethings like baseball, but most is a haze."

"Daniel, God is the father of us all. He is our heavenly father."

"Is that why you always say 'My father, Joseph?' So that all will know you are not referring to the heavenly father?" Daniel asked.

"I was not aware that I did so until you asked me why I do that," Jesus said. "I do not think that it is a bad thing, and both my fathers would understand."

"Why are you so smart, man?" Daniel asked. "How do you know all that you know? Who teaches you? When? Where? It seems that ever since I got here, we have been together. So how do you learn all that stuff that is in your head and in your heart? All the goodness that you want us to practice and live by?"

"I do not have a ready answer for you, Dan. For now, I will have to say I am that I am in Gods will."

CHAPTER 15

One day after Jesus and Daniel had been in the shop assisting Joseph and they were no longer needed, Daniel placed a short, smooth slab of wood back on a shelf. He turned to Jesus and said, "When we get to wherever we will go from here, remind me to tell you about boards on wheels."

Jesus then said, "Let us go down to the oasis and sit for a time. It is early, but perhaps some of our friends will find their way there also."

They sat and shared a pocketful of dried dates that Jesus had brought from home. Shortly there after, Abraham and Levi arrived.

Levi said to Jesus, "Your father, Joseph, told us that you two would probably be here."

Daniel turned his head to his right and shot a look at Jesus.

"Whoa, Levi, how come you said to Jesus 'Your father, Joseph?' What other father would there be?"

"That is what Jesus says when he is talking about his father. He always says Joseph after he says my father. Why? You must ask him."

Daniel recalled his conversation with Jesus on that ubject. Jesus had said that God in heaven was the father of us all. "So we all have two fathers."

"Daniel," Jesus began, "you said I was to remind you to talk about boards on wheels. Tell us now."

"OK. I will tell you what I remember about that. The boards, as I recall, were around three or four feet long." He held out his hands to symbolize the approximate length. "And they had small wheels on the underside."

"That is very small," said Abraham. "Too small to carry anything one could carry by hand. What then were those boards for?"

"You know," started Daniel, "I remember some stuff—some things and only sometime—but not everything. Well, I pretty much do remember everything about baseball.

"Anyway, what I remember about a skateboard is that you put a foot on it and push off with the other to get rolling. Oh yeah, I said that the boards had wheels, huh? But the wheels were not made of wood, they were made of harder stuff. When you got your board moving fast enough, you got on with both feet to ride it."

"We could make them in my father's shop," said Jesus.

Daniel held up a finger and said, "I am not sure that small wheels will roll very well on dirt. Not with the weight of one of you on the board."

"But you said that is what you did," Levi said.

"Yes," said Daniel. "Let me close my eyes and think. Maybe I can remember how we did it."

The boys hushed and let Daniel ruminate.

Some time went by, and then Daniel opened his eyes and spoke.

"OK, something came through. It's not very clear, but I will tell you what I saw. The board was rolling on a hard surface with somebody on it. Not on hard dirt, but something else. I'll close my eyes and maybe I will see more. You all be quiet now."

All were completely silent for nearly fifteen minutes, and then Joshua whispered, "I think he is asleep!"

Daniel popped his eyes open and said, "I heard that, Josh. I was not sleeping and something did come through to me. The hard surface the board was rolling on was gray in color. Do you guys know what gray is?"

All the boys nodded yes.

"And before that, the board, with someone on it, had been rolling on some black stuff," Daniel continued.

"So what was the gray and what was the black stuff?" asked Levi.

"I don't know," Daniel replied. "Maybe it will come to me later. Maybe in my sleep. You know what, dudes? I have now been on the back of an ass," Daniel said to his friends. "Now I would like to find out how it feels to be on a camel."

Abraham told him that being on a camel was uncomfortable and no fun.

"But," he said, "if you so desire, my father has a saddle, and he will let us use it so you can experience riding a camel. We will use one of our camels. Father will want to see that."

They all went over to Abraham's house. His father was an adobe brickmaker and worked behind their house.

"Father," Abraham said, "Daniel has not ever been on a camel and he wants to see what it feels like."

"All right," the father said. "Get one saddled, and get Daniel up on it. Then call me. I want to see this."

Daniel sat in the saddle as he was told: sidesaddle with his right leg hooked over the saddle horn. When he was situated properly, he said, "OK," and Abraham led him twice around the house.

"Whoa, whoa," exclaimed the thoroughly bounced and trounced lad on the camel. "This is not cool, man. I want off! I get it now. The Tuaregs that we have seen come through here are on camels because that is what they are used to, probably from birth."

Mathew, Abraham's father, stepped forth and helped Daniel dismount.

"So, Daniel, how many camels will you own when the time comes? If you come here daily and ride, in time, you will be a fair match for any camel rider. Maybe even a Tuareg."

With a slinky eye aimed at Mathew, Daniel said, "No, no, no! It's not going to happen. My camel riding days are over, Mathew."

His friends were giggling up a storm. Mathew joined them and then hugged Daniel.

"You did well and looked just fine in the saddle," Mathew told him.

The next day arrived and Jesus had only one item to deliver to a customer. It was light and could be carried in his arms. After the delivery, Jesus and Daniel would be on their own.

Along the way to the customer's residence, Daniel asked of Jesus, "Do you have any plans for the rest of our day?"

Jesus walked in silence for a short time. Then he spoke.

"I am going to try and gather people at a place where I can talk to them."

"What will you talk to them about, Jesus?"

"The very same things I was speaking to the teachers and doctors in the Temple in Jerusalem about, Daniel."

"But it sure looked like they weren't listening. It looked like they wanted to shut you up. Looking at them, I got the feeling that some wanted to grab you up and throw you right out. I really think that didn't happen because, just in time, your father, Joseph, and your mother came into the Temple and got us out of there. Say, come to think of it, do you think if they had grabbed you and chunked you out that they would have done the same to me?"

Jesus stopped walking and turned to Daniel with a smile across his twelve-year-old face and a gleeful twinkle in his eyes.

"Yes, Daniel, I do believe you would have been with me all the way."

CHAPTER 16

They walked on farther into Nazareth, which because it had less than five hundred inhabitants qualified it as a village rather than a town, until they approached the marketplace. There they found a gathering of children. They ranged in age from five to maybe ten to twelve.

Jesus went near them and just stood there quietly. Daniel stood nearby and was also silent. Shortly thereafter, the eight to ten kids stopped doing what they were into and just stood there and looked at Jesus.

Jesus said, "Would you like to hear a story?"

"Yes," said one and all.

Jesus told them about a friend of his who had never gone to Jerusalem until a few days past. He told them of what he and his friend had done there. He also told them that his friend had insisted on riding a camel and then could not wait to get off.

The kids all laughed at that. Then one of them told Jesus, as all of the children looked at Daniel, that a small group of desert people were camped just outside of the village.

"If your friend would like to ride a camel again, the Tuaregs are friendly and would let him."

All along, Daniel had been aware that the story Jesus told about Jerusalem and the camel ride had been about him. He though it would be kind of interesting to meet and talk with the desert people, but he was not going to ride a camel again—ever.

Daniel said to Jesus, "Dude, if you do want to go talk with the desert people, well, OK, let's do it. But I am not getting on any camel. Nope, not gonna, man!"

Jesus patted Daniel on his back and told him he didn't have to, but if he changed his mind, it would be OK.

Several of the kids asked Jesus if he would come back soon and talk with them again. He told them that he would anytime he was not needed in his father's, Joseph's, carpentry shop.

"What will you talk about to the desert people?" Daniel asked Jesus. "Please don't tell them about my camel ride."

"I will talk to them about doing the right things for themselves and all others and to help where needed—in whatever way possible—to mend the suffering and hurt of others."

Daniel looked closely at Jesus. He then shook his head and said, "Tell me the truth, are you really just twelve years old? 'Cause if anyone should ask me, I would have to say that you've got to be like old—twenty or more."

"No, Dan, you can tell anyone who should ask that I am indeed twelve. Come. Let us go and find the Tuaregs—the desert people. I promise that I will not tell them how you love to ride camels."

"Why do they ride camels? They are rough riders. Why not use asses instead?" Daniel asked seriously.

"Daniel," said Jesus, "they come from far away across a big dessert. Asses need water, camels not as much, and they can carry a bigger load."

They headed out in the direction pointed out to them by the kids that Jesus had spoken with. Less than ten minutes later, they located the Tuaregs encampment. Jesus went straight to their campfire where they were all gathered for their meal.

"Hello," he said to them. "Welcome to Nazareth."

Daniel was introduced, and then Jesus introduced himself. They were welcomed to the campsite and asked to share in their meal. Jesus and Daniel accepted some food, which they were told was dried and smoked camel and goat meat. They both ended up agreeing that it was indeed very favorable.

In due time, Jesus had the full attention of all in the camp, including Daniel. Jesus was speaking pretty much what he had said to the kids earlier.

Daniel thought, *He is really good at this. He will probably grow up to be a teacher, maybe like the ones he tried to talk with at the Temple in Jerusalem. I bet when he is thirty or so people will listen. What he is saying is good stuff.*

When Jesus appeared to be through with what he wanted to convey to his audience, the apparent leader of the desert people spoke. He told Jesus

Daniel T. Reese and the Prophet King

that what he had said to them was how they, all the desert people, lived. He said that because of the way he had preached to them, Jesus would surely grow up to became a prophet among his people.

When Jesus and Daniel said good-bye to the desert people, their leader asked if they would like a camel ride to their home.

CHAPTER 17

On the way back to Jesus's home, Daniel said, "You do have the gift of gab—um, that means that you sure can talk up a storm." Daniel glanced over at Jesus. Jesus was looking at Daniel with a "What you talking about?" look on his face.

Daniel stopped walking and Jesus did also. "What I mean is that what you said to the desert people sure had their interest. What their leader said about you is surely true, except the part that you will be a prophet among your people when you grow up. As far as I am concerned, man, you are a prophet now. Probably born one, dude. Not only can you get a bunch of us kids to listen and pay attention to you but also you did it with the desert people. They took in every word."

When their evening meal was over, Jesus and Daniel went out and once again took their positions against the outer house wall.

Jesus was the first to speak. "Daniel, have you remembered anymore about your family, friends—anything at all? What did you do there, other than play baseball and ride boards with wheels?"

"You know, Jesus, it's funny that you should mention boards with wheels. Something has been kicking around in my head for a couple of days that has something to do with that, but in passing. Like smoke on the water. You can feel that it is water by touching it but you cannot see it because the smoke hides it. I feel that those boards with wheels—that is, something about them in my thoughts tells me—may have something to do why I am here.

"And no, Jesus, I have not had any thoughts or visions about my family or friends. It almost feels like I never left them. I know that they are there somewhere. I do have to figure out how to get back to where I came from though."

Jesus was momentarily somber and quiet. After a few minutes passed, he turned to Daniel and spoke.

"I have a very strong feeling that you're leaving here will soon come to pass. I will not look forward to having you gone, Daniel, but I will accept that what will be will be."

"I suppose that you are correct, but how did I get here, Jesus, and how am I to get back?"

"I feel certain that something will happen, and you will find yourself back where you are from. You might not even recall that you have been here," Jesus replied.

"Yeah, right, like I could totally forget you and the other guys, or Joseph, Mary, James, and Salome. Sure, I'll leave here and never ever give it another thought!" Daniel said and shot a slink eye at Jesus.

Jesus reached over and once again placed his right hand on Daniel's head and then ruffed his hair. "You will be so glad and joyful to be back home and with your father, mother, brothers, and sisters—if you have any—Dan. Maybe you are an only child."

"Don't say that about me maybe being an only child. I want what you have: a James and Salome. Like that, man."

They were both quiet for a time. They watched the stars come out and twinkle in the cloudless sky.

"What have you to do tomorrow in the shop?" Daniel asked.

"My father has not said anything to me about that. Usually he tells me what I am to do the next day—help in the shop and or deliver a finished product to a customer. I suppose I am not needed in the shop tomorrow, and my mother has not said anything about doing errands or anything else for her. Why do you ask, Dan?" "How about we do a walkabout out there in the hills? I have yet to get a good look around. You know when I get back to where I came from, surely I will be asked where I was and what it was like there. Yes, we went outside of town, but we didn't go very far. How about we go over hill and dale so I can get a good look around and get a real feel for your surroundings?

Makes me wish I had a camera."

That last comment got a sideways look from Jesus.

"What is a camera, Daniel?" Jesus asked.

"What you talking about?" said Daniel.

"A camera," Jesus said. "You said you wished you had one."

"I did? I don't remember saying that, man. I don't know what that is, and if I ever did, I don't know now. Do you?" Daniel asked Jesus who again was looking at him through the twelve-year-old eyes of his time.

"Tomorrow we will head out after the morning meal and go—how did you say it? Oh, I remember: over hill and dale so you can get a good feel of where you are," Jesus said.

The following morning, Jesus asked Joseph and Mary if he and Daniel were free to go exploring. They were told that they were.

On their way out of Nazareth, the boys came across a group of kids approximately their age. Two or three of them hollered, "Hey, Jesus, come talk to us for a while. Some of these fellows have not heard you before. We have told them some of what you said to us the other day, and all of us want to listen to you again."

Jesus looked to Daniel.

"Go ahead, talk to them. You are good at it, and what you say—not just to kids but to all—is really good stuff, man. We have time, and besides, I like to listen to you too." Daniel said and then gave Jesus a gentle push toward the kids. "Go on, dude, and tell them about your talk with the Tuaregs and how you captured their full attention."

Jesus asked a few questions of the group in general. Things like what they liked to do when they had free time, together or alone. He went on to tell them about showing goodness to all and to themselves, and how to go about it. Then he asked if any of them had heard about baseball. When it was established that no one had, Jesus told them that one day soon he and Daniel would return and teach them how to play the game. Of course, they all wanted to learn about baseball and how to play it. Daniel smiled and thought that they were gonna like it big ime.

CHAPTER 18

On Daniel and Jesus went up into the surrounding hills and through whatever underbrush and shrubbery they encountered. Here and there, they came across wildlife: deer, antelope, birds, foxes, coyotes, and wolves.

Daniel grabbed Jesus by his right arm and said, "How about you tell me how many times you've come out here, and what you do to them? The animals, I'm saying, man. I know for a fact that if you were not with me, I would be wolf meat. They are wild wolves, right?"

"Yes, Daniel, they are not pets," Jesus told him.

"Why are they like this around you? The first time I saw this, I thought that somehow you had befriended them before. That was then, dude, but this time we are at a different place, right? These are all different animals, right? You have never been with them before, right? So why aren't they attacking? Like, why aren't the wolves all over the deer and the antelope, or us, man? They look at you as if you are their long lost daddy. They aren't acting at all like they're supposed to be. Weird, dude!

"What is it about you? It seems to me that I am sort of different, too, since I met you. You know? It feels good. I am glad to know you and that only good will come of it. The animals probably feel that way around you also."

As they continued to walk along, Daniel kept a close eye on Jesus. He looked very happy and serene—angelic. *He is only twelve,* Daniel thought. *He certainly sounds much older, and how does he know about what he says? I don't really know what a prophet is and why that one desert man told Jesus that he would be a prophet for his people, but if a prophet is way smart, man, his people already have a prophet. He is the one! He is it! He is one smart dude.*

Later, after the evening meal, Jesus and Daniel met with Abraham, Joshua, and Levi back at the town's watering hole. Daniel told their friends about Jesus talking with the kids and then with the desert men. He also went on and on about the animals and how they were with Jesus and him too.

"The wolves would surely have attached me if he hadn't been there with me. When I go back to where I came from—if I ever do—I'm going to miss you guys. I do like it here, but I have this weird feeling that it is way different from where I came from. How and why I can't put my finger on it. I just know that the difference is there. I'm gonna miss all of you and all of this."

Levi said, "If you ever leave us, Dan, we will miss you too. As time goes by, just think of all the things that you remember about where you came from and then tell us about them. Who knows what will come to you, maybe a lot of useful things that would make our lives better and more enjoyable and fulfilling. When are you going to teach Mary, Jesus's mother, how to make dogs hot?"

"Are you in a hurry to get back to your home, Daniel?" asked Abraham.

"It is not so much that I am in a hurry to get back; it's that deep down inside me, I know that somehow I am living two lives. Somehow, I just know that I am in two places at the same time. I do very much like it here, and having you all as friends is really cool. You have families—fathers, mothers, brothers, and sisters. Even if I do not remember them, I know that I do too. How did I get here? Why am I here? Am I supposed to be here forever?"

No one responded. The clear sky was vibrating with the twinkling of stars that filled the moonless vastness from horizon to horizon.

Jesus reached out and placed a hand softly on Daniel's back. "Daniel," he quietly stated, "we all, and I do mean all of us, will miss you when you are no longer here. My mother will especially, for she looks upon you as being hers. One day, Daniel, you will go home."

Daniel gazed at Jesus. "How old are you, really?" he asked his friend.

***

Local hospital one day after Daniel's accident.

Joey Nape entered the second-floor hospital room, number 215, followed by three other boys. He went right up to Daniel's parents.

"Good morning, Mr. and Mrs. Daniels," Joey said.

Both parents looked up from their chairs. Mrs. Daniels said, "Good morning, Joey, and the rest of you boys. How did you get here and so early?"

"My father brought us. He said that he was going to the cafeteria for a cup of coffee so that we could visit with Daniel. He will come up a little later. How is he? Has he woken up yet? Joey asked. "He had an ugly gash in his head that was bleeding a lot. I tried to stop it with my T-shirt, but it wasn't doing much good after it got soaked."

Joey continued, "Its' a good thing Mrs. Riley was out weeding her garden. She saw it happen and called 911. He is going to be all right, isn't he?"

Mr. Reese answered, "Yes, Joey, he will be fine. The doctor shaved a spot on his head so he could stitch up the cut. It took three stitches. The X-rays showed no other damage, but the doctor told us that he is in a coma and may have a concussion. He could be out for a few days. There's no way to tell how long.

"Yeah," Mr. Reese continued, "It looks really bad because of all the bandages wrapped around his head, but we pray that he will heal and be himself once more. We love him the way he was: a good son."

"Yeah, Mr. Reese, we all like him that way too. I hope that he won't want to give up skateboarding. He was getting good at it. He nearly jumped that curb."

CHAPTER 19

"Look, look," one of the other boys shouted. "He moved! Danny moved his left arm."

Daniel's eyes popped open, and he turned his head to take in all that was around him.

"What's up?" Daniel asked. "Why are you people here in my bedroom?"

Mouths dropped open all around. Joey Nape was the first to get his tongue working, and he responded, "This is not your bedroom, dude. You are in a hospital and we all are here to visit you and see if you are doing OK."

"A hospital? Why am I in a hospital?" asked a highly perturbed Daniel.

"Honey," Mrs. Reese said as she reached over and took Daniel's hand in both of hers. "You fell and hit your head on the sidewalk."

Daniel's father held Daniel's other hand tenderly in his.

"Mrs. Riley saw it happen, and when she saw that you were bleeding and unconscious, she called 911," Daniel's mother told him.

Daniel removed his right hand from his father's grasp and reached up to touch his head. "If I hit my head on the sidewalk hard enough to cut me and knock me out, why doesn't it hurt? Mom, you said I was bleeding. Did I get stitches?"

"Yes, you did," said Mr. Reese. "The doctor shaved around the cut and put in three stitches."

"Cool!" Daniel exclaimed. "I wanna see them."

"Yeah, yeah!" the boys said in unison.

Daniel immediately began tugging at the bandages around his head. He got one end to unravel, and soon his head was free.

Mrs. Reese was the first to react. She put both hands to her mouth. "My dear Lord!" she blurted.

"What? What's the matter?" Mr. Reese asked as he turned to his wife. Everyone else in the room was silently staring at Daniel's parents.

"What is it, Mom? Are you sick?" asked an astonished Daniel.

"My God! My God! Look at Danny's head! Look where the doctor shaved him. There are no stitches, no cut, no swelling, and the hair is back. It's a miracle."

They all stared at Daniel's head. Daniel looked at them, each in turn and asked, "What the heck, Mom?"

The other boys and Mr. Reese crowded in close to Daniel to check out his head. The boys, of course, had seen Daniel take the header into the sidewalk that knocked him unconscious and caused severe bleeding.

"Danny," Mr. Reese said, "you had an accident while skateboarding. You were knocked out and bleeding from a nasty gash in your head. An ambulance brought you to the hospital, son."

"Really, Dad? An ambulance? How cool is that, huh?"

"Daniel," his mother said, totally mesmerized, "you were seriously hurt. You did have a gash in your head. The doctor told us that you were in a coma, and he didn't know for how long. And Danny, he did put in three stitches to close up your scalp."

"Yeah right! Why are all of you doing this?" Daniel exclaimed. "If what you say happened, why don't I at least have a headache? There is no pain, no bruise, no stitches. My head is not shaved anywhere. The only thing I remember is that we, the guys and me, were skateboarding. Now this! You guys set it all up, huh? Why? Is it some sort of joke all of you are pulling on me? And if so, why? It must have cost a lot if I really am in a hospital—and did I really ride in an ambulance?"

While Daniel was going through his spiel, his father had quietly left the room and now returned with the doctor who had stitched Daniel up in tow.

"Excuse me, please," the doctor said as he beckoned Mrs. Reese, Joey Napes, and the other boys to move out of his way. He was more than anxious and intrigued. Daniel's father had located him and told him that he must see Daniel because of the way the boy was acting. The doctor was, of course, considerably skeptical of what he had been told, but it was his duty to check it out.

"Who did this?" the doctor asked. "Who has been here since I was? Since we X-rayed you, and I shaved your head and stitched you up?"

"Beats me," said Daniel. "I guess I was asleep. I don't know anything."

"Well," said the highly indignant doctor, "I don't know who but somebody did something."

"Did what?" asked Daniel.

"Healed your gashed and swollen head after removing the stitches that I put in," said the doctor forcefully.

"Yeah, sure, doc! And then what? The person glued some hair and covered the spot you shaved?" asked a grinning Daniel.

All eyes in the room were steadily fixed on the doctor.

"I don't know, son," the doctor replied. "I certainly don't know who is responsible for this. What can you tell me about it? Did you see anyone come in here? During the night, perhaps?"

Everyone in the hospital room with Daniel T. Reese fell completely silent and focused on him intently.

Daniel looked directly overhead for several long minutes and then spoke. "At this time, I know for sure that I was skateboarding with the guys. That is it. I don't remember anything else. There is this, though: I have this sensation that someone put a hand on my head and ruffled my hair. That's it. How could I have had an accident with a cut head that required shaving my head and stitches and then the very next morning all of that is gone like nothing happened? And which one of you had your hand on my head and ruffled my hair? Was it you, Mom? Or you, Dad?"

No one in the room spoke for several moments that passed as if each were an eternity. Finally, Mr. and Mrs. Reese said at the same time, "No, Daniel, I didn't."

Daniel turned to the doctor. "And what do you have to say about this? No gash, no shaved spot, and no cut! So exactly what did you do to me? Yeah, yeah, there is blood on the bandages, but it can't be mine, right? Where did you get them—the bloody bandages? And why would you want to fake this? Oh, yeah, more money, huh? How much per stitch, doc?"

"Wait a minute here, young man. I did not fake anything. You came in here bleeding and unconscious. Several others saw you like that—before I shaved your head and stitched you up and afterward. Then you were thoroughly X-rayed and examined by others."

"Uh huh! Sure, sure, doc. So where is the damage that you cared for when I got here? Do you have special powers that you can make a cut go away and no one can tell it was ever there? Did anyone help you when you worked on me?" asked Dan.

"Yes, sure. A nurse was here with us. I will have her come in and talk with you. I now want your parents' permission to draw some of your blood. I will send it to our lab for analysis and have them do the same with the blood that is on the dressing of your wound. We can also have them do DNA comparison to prove, once and for all, that you did indeed suffer a gash in your head from your skateboard accident."

Daniel looked to his parents. They nodded their heads in agreement.

CHAPTER 20

The doctor assured Daniel and his parents that he would see to it that all the tests would be taken care of. They would only be charged for the X-rays and the room. The ambulance was a separate thing. He would notify them when the lab finished with the testing.

"Daniel," the doctor said, "we will need to take a swab sample from inside your mouth. Then—"

"Oh wow, Mom and Dad!" Daniel shouted. "Just like in cop shows!"

"Neat! Cool! Yowza! Dude!" exclaimed his young friends.

"Mr. and Mrs. Reese, one of you will have to sign some consent paperwork," the doctor said. "Then when Daniel is dressed, you are free to take him home."

"So, doctor, even if the blood on the bandages is proven to be mine," Daniel asked, "there is still no cut, no stitches, no bump, and no shaved spot. What do you think? How can all this be as it is?"

The doctor stood pensive and immobile. He looked directly at Daniel and shook his head. Then he quietly and slowly said, "I don't know, son, and I can't even began to guess. Your mother probably got it right; it must be a miracle."

Daniel looked all around and then he asked, "Mom, did you guys bring me some clean clothes? I bet that if I really was bleeding as much as Joey said, I probably shouldn't wear what I had on during the accident."

***

"Come on, Mom! So I took a spill the other day, but as you can plainly see, there's no damage. I will be more careful now, and I won't try to jump any curbs again. If I want to go up on the sidewalk, I will get off my board and carry it. I promise, Mom," Daniel said. "So can I go with the guys? Please!"

It was a beautiful August day in Vancouver, Washington. Daniel's friends were gathered in the Reese's front yard, ready to roll. Mrs. Reese looked lovingly at her son, took him in her arms, and hugged him close and tight. "All right, Daniel, you may go, but promise that you will not—I say again, not—try that curb trick again. Ever!"

"I promise, Mom. Never, ever will I try it again. Something saved me once, but I don't want to chance it again," Daniel said as he walked toward the front door. He stopped, turned, and then ran back to his mother and wrapped his arms around her waist. He looked her straight in the eye and said, "You are the best mom anyone could want. You have just reminded me of another mother I think I met somewhere, but I don't know where or when. Thank you, Mom. I love you from here to eternity."

Then Daniel let go of his mother and dashed out to be with his friends.

***

First thing Daniel did when he was outside in front of his waiting buds was to holler out and got all their attention.

"I got something to tell you all and I need your fullest attention. All of you – if not all then most – were with me when what happened to me happened. I blew the jump onto the curb and knocked myself out." So do you guys know who said that? That part' no more forever!

"My dad was reading a book about Pacific Northwest Indians and I picked it up one day from the chair where he had left it. I read thru it some and I came to the part where the chief of the Nez Perce Indians said 'I will fight no more forever.'

"Don't you guys get on me about curb jumping. I told my mother that I will jump no curbs forever. You dudes got that?"

All his friends there with him had seen him knocked out and laying in his blood. They all assured him that they would not press him to do anything that he did not want to do.

They honored his word to the fullest – no curb jumping talk. As the morning waned so did the skate boarding enthusiasm, The boys found a tree in a neighbor's yard that threw enough shade for all six of them and they happily took to it. The house owner did not mind. He told them that they were welcome as long as they minded the flower beds and they did not leave trash behind.

Once they were all hunkered down and settled Joey turned to Daniel and got his attention. So, Danny, What do you think happened the other day? We – most all of us – saw you take the fall. And – we all saw you knocked out and bleeding. Other people saw you like that, too, man.

"Then when you woke up the next day---no bumps, no stitches, no shaved spots and no cut. Weird, huh? Can we talk about it?"

Daniel sat quiet and pensive for a time. Then he looked at all his friends – they were all riveted on him. He shrugged his shoulders, held out both his hands – palms up and said, "I do not know how to even begin to explain about my supposed head injury. I do accept what you all have told me of how it happened but I do not remember any of it – not before and certainly not after. All I know is that I woke up to a room full of people and in a hospital,"

Paul, one of the boys hunkered there, spoke up. "Danny, while you were out of it did you not hear, see or talk to any one while you were knocked out? I have an aunt that is a nurse in a hospital. She has told us – my family – that several people that were knocked out for some time or were in a coma that when they woke up they talked about where they had been and who they had met there and talked with. Didn't you do anything like that, man?"

"No, Paul. I don't think so but maybe, huh? I will think on it. May be something will surface," Daniel said.

"So – we got time now," said Arthur. "Just close your eyes and concentrate. We will all shut up while you send yourself back in time. To when you were gone – not here with us after you took that header. Where did you go to? Where were you? Did you talk with anyone there? Think, Danny, Think!!"

"Ok, guys. I'll give it a go. Maybe Paul and Art are right and I may have something locked up in my gourd. If I try really hard maybe I can grab' on to something that I will share with you. Quiet please – not a sound!!

All went totally quiet and still. No breeze to rustle the trees. No birds singing or chirping. Traffic – both foot or vehicular – must, too, have a dead stop. Not a sound was heard – at least not by Daniel T Reese. He had willed his consciousness to dredge up any and all memories of his past.

After fifteen minutes had elapsed Daniel opened his eyes. His pal, Joey, could not have stood it any. If Danny had not come to life just then Joey was all for shaking him back.

"Okey, okey, dude – what? What did you see? What do you know now man?" Joey screamed at his friend.

Daniel looked around taking in all of his friends. He could see that they all were super anxious to know what he had recalled.

"All I remembered was when I was a little kind. When I got my tricycle, and when I got my first bike and my dad teaching me to ride it. Stuff like that – you know? One thing tho, there were donkeys out in the street. Where? I don't know. I looked around but could not tell where."

"Aw, man! I think I might know where," Bobby hollered out. There in a town up in the hills in Arizona – my dad took us, the whole family, to that town. Let me see, um? Oh, yeah, man! The town is named OATMAN. Why? You might ask. Maybe because they feed all them donkeys – and there is a lot of them – OATS. Ya knows what I mean?"

Randy, another of the boys said, "Bobby, Robert, Bob – I think all of us know what OATS are, Thank you.

"If I did see or was around asses I don't think it was in that town. What? Why are you all looking at me like that?" Daniel asked his friends. "What, dudes?"

Joey was the first to speak. He said, "Daniel, you said asses – like maybe in butts, man!"

"I did not!!" Cried Daniel vehemently. "Did not!!"

"Yes, you did, Joey tell him. Ask any of us. You did."

"Well, if I did I don't know why. What do you think made me do that? What were we talking about, anyway?"

"Bobby told us about a town in Arizona where donkeys are in the street and folks feed them oats. The town is named OATMAN. Remember?" Joey said.

"Yeah, yeah! I do remember. But why would I then say what you say I said? I have not been around any girls for days and days. Have I? I don't remember where I have been might, what I did there and who I might been there with," Daniel told his group of buddies.

"It is only a couple of days since your dive. Maybe in time you might remember where and what you did there then you can fill us in," Joey said. "Bet you had an out – standing time. If it had been lousy you would not want to remember it --- Whoa, whoa." Maybe that is it! You think, dude? Don't wanna remember?"

CHAPTER 21

Time crept by and Daniel's friends pretty much kept mam about his fall, his injury and his mysterious total recovery – which evidently had healed overnight. Yup, overnight and so completely that no single trace or it having happened was left for any to see or acknowledge that it had indeed happened.

That it did happen, a set of parents, a bunch of friends, a neighbor lady, ambulance guys, nurses and at least one doctor and the person that took the X rays, were witness to the undeniable fact that the injury to Daniels head did absolutely and frighteningly happen.

Why had no one – medically speaking – follow up with questioning how and why this overnight complete healing happened.

Daniel mother, at the hospital when first her son had removed the bandages and wrappings from his head and there was no longer evidence of an injury, had then pronounced it a miracle.

Daniel now and again gave thought to all the known facts as he knew them to be. Thinking about it did not bring forth to him any conclusive recollection of what he may have experienced, seen, heard or done. He did now and again be grabbed by a distant thought or far away and slight memory – smoke like, not entirely solid- that did not ever linger. Maybe one day I will be able to distinguish or comprehend the full meaning of what now and again my mind conjures up.

It happened on the way. Daniel and his parents were on their way to early church service. They lived a minute's walk away so they were taking advantage of the beautiful, sunny Sunday morning. When you live in the Pacific Northwest to do that- love the sunshine when it does.

"Come on, come on!" Daniel's father shouted back at him. He was sauntering several paces behind his parents. He cleared his head and pushed himself to catch up.

Sometime in the middle of the sermon Daniel realized that he had not heard any of it so far.

"What the heck?" he asked himself quietly. "Where was I? And who was I with? And where are we going?"

He somewhat remember – he thought. "There were people walking. But I could only see "them a little. Could not tell what they looked like, what they wore. I think I saw donkeys – I think they could have been."

He all of a sudden was fully back- sitting in church next to his mother and father. When the sermon ended and all had received blessing they filed out and cleared the church. Good byes were exchanged and soon Daniel was left with his parents. As they were about to depart for their home Mrs. Reese grabbed Dan in a tight hug and said to him

"I am so proud of you, Daniel. I saw that you were mumbling. I could not hear or make out what you were saying but I know that you were saying thanks for your miracle. We love you, Danny!!"

"What could I think about what I may have been mumbling? It is a mystery to me – all of it. How did my injury heal all by its' self and over night? How about the stitches, the bump – and the, the hair?" Daniel played that over and again in his brain. "How could that happen?"

The last part came out of his mouth loud and clear but no one was nearby to have heard him.

Again, Daniel T. Reese was only twelve years old. Six months and some days before he would turn thirteen. He did not yet poses the know how to figure it out – not about his fall but after – how, where, why?

A couple of days later Daniel and his pal Joey Napes were at a nearby city park sitting in side by side swings and slurping on chocolate and nuts covered ice cream bars.

They had bought them from the ice cream truck when it had come by. "Remember those?? They now cruise by only in our memories," Joey silently asked himself.

Then his eyes lit up and he turned to Daniel.

"Hey, hey, dude, has anything else come through your gourd about – Aw, man, I gotta say it – your trip? And I do not mean your flight to the sidewalk. Where did you go, man? You musta been somewhere where something or someone did something to fix your split head. It was split, man. I was there and I saw it then next – gone! No trace. Just bloody bandages."

Daniel stopped swinging and talked to his friend, "Joey," he said. I don't know how or why my head healed up. I do believe everybody that my head was split and bleeding. But no I "still do not anything. Sometimes, at anytime and anywhere, my mind goes away but to where is a mystery. I do not have a clear picture of what and why and it does not last long.

"Last Sunday in church I left. I don't mean I got up and split. I my mind I went away. Where to? I could not tell. Could not see clearly – fog, smoke, mist, like that. But I think I saw donkeys. Probably because what Bobby told us about the donkeys in that town in Arizona. What is the name? Has to do with food." Daniel stated.

"OATMAN!" Joey told him. "You mean your gourd took you there? Now how cool is that, man? You see any asses Too?"

"Shut up Joey!" Daniel loudly told him. But he did so with a smile.

Every now and then, Joey would ask again, "Anything yet?" Or it would come up by one or another of his friends when they were together. Though Daniel knew, without a doubt, that what had happened to him on that particular day – and what followed – may never be clear and positive in his mind. But in his heart of hearts he knew that his mother was right when she stated at the hospital when he removed his bandages that it was a miracle.

CHAPTER 22

One early morning Daniel ran out to gather up that day's newspaper. As he jumped off the porch and cleared the shallow two steps he got tangled up in the coiled garden hose. He tripped and fell forward and sideways onto the brick walkway that led to the rear of the house. He received a nasty scratch on his right arm. He got himself up right, looked at his arm and acknowledged that indeed there was a slightly seeping and red scratch.

"Oh, man! My mom is gonna not like this. After my dive into the side walk just a couple of days ago this ain't good." Then he caught himself and realized that he had spoken out loud. He took a quick look around and found no one that could have seen him fall or have heard him speak. Then – luckily he was wearing a long sleeve shirt – he unrolled both sleeves so his parents would not see his scratch.

He went and picked up the newspaper and headed back into the house. "Man! I hope mom or dad did not look out the window and saw me fall," he quietly told himself.

Dan got his newspaper and mom gat a hug and a cheek kiss.

"I'm not hungry right now. I will get a hamburger later with the guys. We made plans yesterday to go to the Dairy Queen today. They got killer burgers there… um, I guess that does not sound right, huh?"

He rushed out of the dining room and headed for his room. In his room Daniel peeled off his shirt – left arm out first then freed his torso with freeing his right arm last. That sleeve had some body fluid on it and it would wash out easily. Now that his right arm was bare Daniel astonishingly acknowledged that there was not a mark on it. He couldn't take his unbelieving eyes away. He had seen the scratch – he had – and he had felt it, too. Now nothing! No pain. No mark's at all – like it had never happened.

Daniel could not help doing it – he swiveled his head in every direction. Looking for what? "Who, what did it? Where is my nasty scratch?" His fevered mind asked.

"No everybody was astonished that my head was healed, "he said out loud to himself. "Maybe it is some change in myself. So I heal up quickly? Like right now – immediately? Now! Something else is happening. But what? It seems that it started with my kissing the sidewalk"

He looked a long look at his right arm again. He could not find even the smallest indication that it had been scraped raw and only a short while ago.

"Weird! I guess I gotta live with it. But I wonder if my hazy visions are tied in. Don't think I wanna thank my gourd on a side walk again – or anywhere else, man!"

Daniel change his shirt and washed off the right sleeve that had been hiding his scratch. He hung it on a chair in his room. On the way out through the kitchen he said goodbye to his folks.

"See you for lunch. Are you guys going to Costco today? If you do, I'll have a hot dog if you bring me one."

Half a block away from home met with Joey.

"Yo!" Where you going?" asked Joey.

"I was going to the park to see if you and some of the other guys were there," Daniel told him.

"I was headed too your house to see if you wanted to go to the park," Joey said. "I guess it is true, huh?"

"What is, dude?" Daniel asked.

"What is what man?" Joey said.

"Aw, man, Joey! You said I guess it is true. What the heck do you mean? What do you guess is true?"

"Oh, that. The saying, Daniel. The saying!"

"Whoa!" exclaimed Joey. "Guess you never heard it, huh. The saying says' Great minds think alike."

Daniel glanced at his friend and shot him a full face grin.

"So, Joey, were you at the park all ready?" ask Dan.

"Yeah I told the guys I was going to get you dude."

"Who all is there? Dan asked.

During all the talk they had kept walking and now they were within a block from the park. Joey said, "Race you there, man!"

"I was just about to say that!" Daniel threw Joey said and took in a flash. Daniel was on his heels in seconds. When they got to the park in a dead heat they got to laughing hard.

The other friends gathered around them. "Who or what chased you?" One guy asked. Made Daniel and Joey laugh harder and longer.

Daniel invited Joey home to have lunch. "It will be cool with my folks, Joey.

Joey pulled out a cell phone and called his home and spoke with his mom and got an okay from her. He told Dan. Daniel said to him, "Let me use your phone and I will call my mom." Joey handed it over to him.

Daniel pumped in the number and spoke with her for just a short while. You are the best. Love you! He handed back to Joey his cellphone.

"Mom said that you are welcome to come with me for lunch. My folks, being that it is Saturday, are together at Costco. We are having big hot dogs for lunch, dude!"

That night, when he was comfortably tucked into bed, Daniel lay wide awake. His thoughts tightly wrapped his fall and the resultant scratch to his right arm. He was becoming kinda used to speaking his thoughts. He caught himself doing it now and he said, "I guess that I am alone and talk softly so no one can hear me then it's cool."

He stopped talking and dwelled his thoughts on what had happened to him this morning. Silently he went on.

"I tripped and fell and hit the brick walkway. There is no doubt about that. My arm was definitely scraped. I felt it. I saw it. So why is there no sign of it now? What is going on here. This is strange for sure, huh?

"Now," he said out loud but softly. "What if everyone that says that they saw my head cut and bleeding after my crash was telling the truth. What the Hey, man!!

His head swirling with unanswered questions, Daniel finely drifted off to sleep. He dreamed that he was in a far off place but he could not tell where. There were people there but he could not tell who. He only saw images – ghost like – shadows, misty.

"Something happened to me after my skateboard crash. I know that I went to the hospital. But where else? Something weird went on while I was knocked out. But what? I now know that my head was cut and bleeding. So where are the stitches? I crashed only a few days ago but there is no trace of injury.

"Every one that knows I was hurt now seem to have just swept it away. What are they covering up. Maybe tomorrow I will come up on something that will lead me to some answers."

Daniel yawned big, turned onto his left side, hugged his pillow and his last thoughts before dropping off were of his left arm, which he now lay his head on, was free and clear of any injury. "Weird stuff."

A couple of days later Joey came to Daniel's house to talk him into going with him to a nearby lake to check out the girls there.

"Why go there?" asked Dan. "There's girls at the park and it is nearer.

"Yeah, dude, but at the lake they are in swim suits," Joey said, "Some are even in two piece, man!"

"Hey! What is up with you lately anyway, man? There are girls everywhere." Daniel said.

"Yeah! But in two piece bathing suits – that's what I'm talking about, Dan! They be looking good, double good, dude. Hey! have you seen anything lately – in your gourd Dan. If so, then talk to me."

Daniel just gave Joey a slinky eye look.

"Alright, alright! Let's go when we get to the lake maybe you will loosen up. What's with you anyway, man? All of us, your friends can tell something is bugging you. Can I help, Daniel??"

"No, Joey. It's just that I am having weird dreams. Dreams of people – maybe people. Since what I see are like shadows I can't tell who they are. Same with where they are. It is all hazy and in shadowy. Not scary, Joey. Just weird, "Said Daniel.

"I know what you mean, Dan. I even know a word for it – Fantasmic.

"Yeah, that fits, Joey"

They got to the park and in no time chose up teams to play baseball.

Joey and Daniel were in opposite teams. Daniel's team won the coin toss so they were up at bat first. Daniel while waiting for his turn at bat suddenly found himself watching a different ball game. Who and where he could not visualize. Soon that all went away just as he was told that he was up to bat.

Later he thought about telling Joey but he realized that he did not have anything to tell but more about shadows. He had nothing solid – only fantastic stuff. "No, I won't say anymore to Joey. Even if I keep seeing stuff. Who would believe any of it. Like my healing almost right after I hurt myself. I have a feeling that, for whatever reason, I will continue to heal - probably for the rest of my life.

"Thank God for that."

CHAPTER 23

Time quickly slipped by and Daniel T Reese finished high school. Went then and served in the military and obtained a four year collage degree after his fulfillment of military tour of duty.

Daniel contacted all his old buddies and invited them to his home on a Saturday for a cook – out and cold beer. That day was extremely perfect. Sunny, no wind and all that were invited showed. All had wives and kids. They all came. Daniels cook – outs were always full - up

Daniel had never married. Was now single, no children and so was available. His Buds, of course, continually tried to get him, as they would say – settled.

"I am now going to tell you guys a story about someone I met while I was searching for an apartment in downtown Portland, Oregon," had Daniel said to Joey and the rest of the gang. "We are going to sit right here in my new digs and eat and drink while I tell you what happened.

"Now this story is about a truly beautiful being inside and out—and I am extremely proud that I met and befriended her. I have to admit, and I am joyful in doing so, that this superb mortal captured my heart. I hope that I do a good job telling you about her so that you might see her through my eyes and feel her love. So here goes. I hope none of it bores you. Just sit back and take it all in. It will do you all good.

"We met now and again by her fountain in Old Town in Portland, down by the river—the Willamette, not the Columbia River. She would tell me about all of her goings and doings. The leaves had begun to lose their coat of summer green. Slowly, yet so quickly, the golden colors of autumn turned them into golden bronze, burnished brass, and tarnished copper. Rain and morning fog appeared with a steady frequency that signaled the onset of winter, but not before the passing of Indian summer.

"It was during that maverick season, sandwiched between summer and winter, and stubbornly interrupting the flow of one season into another, that Portland, Oregon's, finest entered into our world. Amidst the rubble, flotsam, and jetsam beneath one of the many bridges that span the Willamette River in the downtown Portland area, a lone woman wrapped in an array of clothes that consisted of begged, borrowed, and stolen items, painfully and laboriously brought forth a beautiful female child. The mother was an Indian. One of those who made their way into Portland in search of work, a better life, and identity, and end up for several reasons rejected and neglected in Portland's Old Town skid-row streets.

"If it had not been an Indian summer, the child would never have survived. Her receiving blanket was several pages of an old newspaper, and later that day, her only clothing had come from a remnant torn from her mother's ancient, tattered overcoat. Although the mother had not taken good care of herself during the pregnancy, the child had been born wholesome and healthy.

"The mother had no idea who the child's father was. There had been numerous men whom she had been with out of necessity to acquire food and shelter, as well as to drown out the emptiness, the loneliness, and the futility of her life.

"Once the mother had recovered somewhat from the pain and the effort of childbirth, she bundled up the tiny infant as best she could and held her to her breast. As the baby suckled and shared her mother's warmth, the day's misty fog cleared away, providing a view of the moon, which was either late or early in its trek across the Pacific Northwest sky, at ten in the morning. Looking down at her child, the Indian woman gently spoke. 'My beautiful, innocent baby, I have given you life, but I have nothing else to offer you other than a most proper name, which will match your beauty. You shall be called Ramona Day-Moon. Look! Look my baby, is not the beautiful floating there in broad daylight?' Where they lay beneath the bridge, she held the child up toward the open sky.

"The years that followed the girl's birth were lean and hard. Her mother's health, both physical and mental, rapidly deteriorated, and the child was barely looked after. Nevertheless, Ramona Day-Moon grew and flourished. She was a happy child, full of life and wonderment. Seldom was she a bother to anyone, and in fact, even at the very young age of two when she took her first steps, she would find her way to those around her who needed comforting.

"Her world was that of poverty, hunger, and cold. In her meager surroundings, Ramona Day-Moon never knew any luxuries other than those she provided herself from such sources as trash cans and discarded items of clothing, and now and then a broken toy or a half colored-in coloring book.

"The only family she was to ever know consisted of the men and women of skid row. All of them were just as poor, needy, and forgotten as she was. Faces came and went, and with them also went everything that the child had to give. She gave to those who needed anything that she would find and bring with her to wherever she and her mother were staying at the time.

"By the time little Ramona Day-Moon reached her seventh year, she knew every bit of Portland's Old Town. She had learned which grocery stores would throw out fruits and vegetables that had begun to spoil, and she would collect them. Later, she would cut away the rotten portions and distribute the edible leftovers to the old, the crippled, and the very young among her people: bums, winos, and derelicts—lost souls who had found their way to her world.

"Her favorite place was the fountain on the south side of the Burnside Bridge. Not the new fountain of arching aluminum tubes; she liked that one, too, but she loved the old one three blocks further south by the little park alongside the firehouse. It was right in the middle of the crowds that gathered for the Saturday Market. Sometimes a man with a pony cart would be there to sell rides to kids, and once he picked her up and lifted her onto the seat next to him. He didn't take anyone else on that trip, and the two of them went around many streets. The man never spoke to her, only smiled kindly and then gently took her hands and placed them on the reins just above his so that she could get the feel of guiding the horses. For the rest of her life, that ride would be the fullest and happiest time she was to ever experience.

"One day, when she returned to the small, rundown apartment that was shared by eight or ten people who came and went and never remained the same, Ramona found her mother stretched out on the floor and covered with an old tablecloth. She had died several hours before the little girl had come back to her. Someone had gone to find a police officer so that the body could be removed. Someone else took Ramona Day-Moon aside and told her not to say anything or else she, too, would be taken away.

"Through her tears and strangled sobs, the seven-year-old child heard the voice tell her that she could stay there and that she would always have a place to sleep and a free place to come to out of the rain and the cold. The girl was told that her mother would be buried by the city and that there was nothing that anyone could do for her now.

"Confused, frightened, and feeling more alone than ever before, the tiny little girl child slumped into a corner and watched through huge, tear-blurred eyes as the two men in white uniforms placed her mother's body onto a stretcher and took it away forever. The pain in the child's heart was more than she could stand. As she caught a last glimpse of her mother's matted hair spread out beneath the sparkling white sheet, total numbness overtook her, and the child fainted away.

"Several days later, the child's life continued much as it had always been. Ramona Day-Moon went on striving to survive and continued her boundless determination to help those around her. The desire to give of herself, to share with anyone who needed kindness and warmth anything that she had to give or could get, continued. The child's love for everyone and everything came as second nature to her.

"She became aware that certain containers such as soda pop bottles and cans, beer bottles and cans, and even plastic milk cartons had value. Every day, she would take an old tattered "sea bag" and scour the streets, alleyways, and city parks for returnable discards. The money that she received did not go for candy or any kind of sweets for herself. She would take the nickels and dimes and buy canned food or medicine for the sick and the hungry in her skid-row world.

"A day came when a young man drifted into the place where she lived. Cold, hungry, and too sick with the flu to fend for himself, he was soon under the tender care of Ramona Day-Moon. She provided an old but warm blanket to cover him. She brought him fruit and bread, cough syrup, and aspirin, as well as a gentle, loving smile and fathomless compassion.

"The young man slowly regained his health, and as he did so, he began to strum the old guitar that he had carried with him for years. He played soft, soothing music, and he sang pretty songs. Ramona Day-Moon would listen and watch his fingers pick at the strings and slide up and down the long neck of the instrument to form the chords. Sometimes, she would sit perfectly still for hours on end, and the young man knew that she, too, wanted to hold the guitar and make it hum. Not once, though, did the child in anyway let her feelings show. She only exhibited pleasure and a dreamy contentment when he played and sang.

"One morning, the little girl awoke and the young man was gone. His small backpack and navy watch cap were not there either, and she knew that she would never see him again. Laying next to her was a large, irregular object wrapped in the old warm blanket that she had provided to comfort the young man. He had wanted to pin a note to it, but he knew that she could not read. Instead, he left her his most, and only, valued possession. With gratitude and a return of genuine love, he bequeathed to Ramona Day-Moon his guitar!

"Now the little girl could be found every Saturday sitting on the ledge of her favorite fountain right in the middle of the Saturday Market crowds. At first, she would only strum the strings softly as she sat in the morning sun, keeping time to the splashing of the water as it streamed from the fountainheads. Then one day she added her tiny voice to the gentle music, and it was as beautiful and wonderful as the very nature of the child.

"From the very first time that she gave voice to her haunting music, people gathered around, and most would remain for long periods of time, drinking in the sight of the beautiful scene: a lovely tiny girl sitting at the water's edge with the antique fountain rising behind her, with the sound of her guitar strings and her enchanting voice making their spirits soar.

"Someone placed an empty soft drink cup on the fountain ledge alongside the little girl and put several pieces of change it. Within minutes, the cup overflowed with not only an assortment of coins but also dollars, and even one or two five-dollar bills.

"As was her way, at the close of the day, Ramona Day-Moon headed for the little corner grocery store where she always cashed in her bottles and cans. This time, there had been no need to collect returnables. She had more money in her tattered dress pocket than she had ever seen. All totaled, her singing had generated a little over $30, which was enough to purchase two-and-a-half bags of food. She did not forget the new baby down the hall from her grimy apartment. For that week-old infant, Ramona Day-Moon bought cans of condensed milk and a bottle of Karo Syrup. The mother had told her a day before that that was what the baby needed.

"For herself, Ramona Day-Moon bought nothing special. She would share the food with one of the women who lived in her apartment building, who would prepare it on the old hot plate. More than half of the groceries that she bought would be distributed along the way to her needy friends and even those that she had never met, but who looked tired and hungry and helpless. To do this, the child borrowed one of the few shopping carts that the store had. The owner gladly let her take it, for he knew that she would return it right away, and he trusted and liked her.

"On a day-to-day basis, everything remained much the same for Ramona Day-Moon. She would go out and collect usable items of clothing, a pair of shoes now and again, and, of course, all the bottles and cans that she could find. Come Saturday, and then later Sunday also, she would play her music and sing her songs for herself and for all who cared to stop and listen. That old fountain will never be the same without her sitting there on its ledge.

"Not once did the now eight-year-old girl ever think of herself other than to eat when she was hungry and to put on an extra piece of clothing when she felt cold. She knew that better things existed; she saw them in store windows and on the people who went to the Saturday Market. She liked those nice things. She liked how the men and women, the boys and girls, looked in their clean clothes that fit them well and did not have patches or torn spots. She admired the shining new shoes and the various types of sneakers with no holes in them. She fully acknowledged the fact that there were a lot of nice and pretty things in life—things that she did not have, things that no one she knew had. What she did not know was that she, too, could have those things someday. Never did she covet or in anyway envy those who had what she did not. Her life was full—made so by her giving, her helping, and her love for all and everything around her.

"Her eighth year came and went, and then in the winter of 1978 and 1979, when there was snow that lasted for several days, Ramona Day-Moon became ill and weak with cold and hunger. No longer was the Saturday Market active, for after Christmas, it is too cold until March or April to have crafts and food booths out in the open. Now the child had to depend solely on the deposit money from bottles and cans. There weren't too many to be found, and she had to venture out far and for long periods of time to fill her sea bag. More often than not, she appeared at the corner grocery store late in the evening, cold and tired, and with only a third of her sack filled with returnables. Still, Ramona Day-Moon gave away most of what the deposit money bought. Her strong, unfailing determination to do for others continued to take her out early each day and kept her out late with her searching.

"All too fast, her illness turned into pneumonia, but still she went out daily to make her rounds. She became gaunt from the loss of weight, and her normally clear eyes became hazy; her beautiful face was marred with sickly blue-black circles that developed under her eyes, and all the color drained from her body.

"In early 1979, a heavy ice storm hit Portland during the night. The following morning gave light to a scene of destruction yet sheer beauty. Everything was coated with nearly an inch of sparkling ice. The weight of it had broken trees, power lines, and poles. Falling objects had damaged automobiles and buildings. Streets and roads were blocked throughout the entire Portland area, and it was cold!

"There was an old, old man staying in the little girl's apartment and he, too, had come down with pneumonia. Ramona Day-Moon had already been caring for him as best she could, but he got worse each day. She knew that he must have some type of medicine and hot food: soup and maybe some fruit juice. Bundling herself up in all that she had in the way of clothing, the child, now nine years old, took her old sea bag and went out into that morning of ice.

"Ramona Day-Moon made her way through the streets and parking lots, through city parks and alleyways. Her pace was slow and labored because of the ice and her illness, but she searched on and on. By nightfall, she had collected only a handful of cans and bottles, yet the small weight of them slowed her even more.

"As the city lights began to blink on, the child found herself in a small park along the Willamette River. Weak and exhausted, she realized that she would not be able to reach home that night. The natural good health that she had been born with had carried her through bad colds and the flu in the past, but not this time. This time the pneumonia, her greatly congested lungs, and the searing pain in her chest robbed her tiny body of all its strength. She could not go much further.

"Crawling on her hands and knees over the ice on the grass, dragging along her precious cargo of cans and bottles, Ramona Day-Moon made her way to a nearby bridge. That bridge afforded little shelter, and by fate or sheer coincidence, it was the very same bridge under which her mother had lain and given life to her. Huddled up in that very same spot, half frozen by the numbing cold, shivering uncontrollably, and feverish and totally alone, the girl thought only of the sick old man that she would not be able to help.

"Ice extended from the banks for several yards over the river and added to the cold radiated by the steel and concrete of the bridge structure. As the biting cold and the boiling fever overtook her, all feeling began to leave the child's tiny body. No longer did she feel the terrible pain in her chest or the bone-crushing cold. She did not feel the emptiness or the loneliness that surrounded her. She felt only an extreme serenity and peace as her small life ebbed out of her.

"Ramona Day-Moon saw a deep darkness before her, deeper than any she had ever known. Then she began to see light that became soft and bright, warm and soothing. She felt the touch of kindness and gentleness and love for the first time in her existence as the angel embraced her with his gossamer wings. He had come and sat momentarily alongside her to return to her some of the comfort that she had so readily given to others all her life. He had come to Earth to enfold her in his goodness. Ramona Day-Moon looked up into his face and gazed deeply into his loving eyes. She saw in them a better life—the one that she always knew was waiting for her. With her last breath, she smiled her lovely child's smile.

"The angel gathered her up in his arms and carried her off to a place where she would be loved and cherished forever and ever. He had come down from heaven to claim Portland's finest!

"Short, short story, yes. Ramona Day-Moon's life was not only short but also devoid of all but her devotion to caring for others. Her entire world during her short stay on Earth was only a square mile or so. Yet so much was she that, for me, the bright beauty of Earth dimmed with her passing. So much was she that Michael—the archangel—insisted on fetching her home himself.

"This is only one of many, many stories—happy, sad, tragic, and so on—that are the makeup of humanity. There are so many that even I cannot account for them all.

"Ramona Day-Moon's first day on Earth was under a bridge swaddled in newspaper and a scrap of cloth, but, oh, I wish you could have seen her. Her life was short, and those of us outside looking in may feel that it was harsh and sad. She felt otherwise. It gave her happiness to be able to help anyone in need, and she saw her world as a worthy place. Rather than complain or feel sorry for herself, she felt contentment.

"Telling her story places my heart in a vise, but you know what? When I am allowed, I rejoice in being with her and visit with her where she now resides.

"She really did exist and this poem is for her.

In the hush of a new day dawning
Or at its end,
Gazing into a clear day or starlit night
Now and then,
A small and fragile gentle bird
Through my memory in silence
Makes her flight.
The flutter of her wings touch
Here and there, oh so lightly,
Slowly and sweetly,
One feather at a time.
The treasures buried in my mind
She coaxes from recesses and crevices
Held there tightly,
All the images, thoughts, and deeds,
That she can find.

"So ends the story of Ramona Day-Moon. She was one of a kind for sure, and again I say how happy and enthralled I am to have know her," Daniel said.

Joey replied, "How come all this cool and amazing stuff happens to just you?"

"You know, Joey, I too, have often thought and pondered upon just that, and I don't have an answer," Daniel said. "I am extremely grateful that my life is what it has been. All of us have been very fortunate. We have wonderful families that love us, and at our age, we are all very close in that we all are pretty well set. All of us have great educations and great jobs and good incomes. So how can you, Joey Napes, say that cool stuff happens to just me? Look at you. You have a beautiful wife and two wonderful kids—a boy and girl only a year apart. Now, is that not the coolest of the cool?"

"Yeah, Joey," the other three friends shouted in unison. They, too, were happily married and two others had children.

"Hey, hey!" shouted Joey. "How come you have never married, Daniel? You do like woman, right? Please, please say that you do. If not, we men will still hang out with you. Won't we, guys?"

No one said anything for a long couple of minutes.

"Well," said a smiling Daniel, "I always thought that you, Joey, were cute as a button. Come to me and give me a big hug."

All four boys—men now—backed away from Daniel with wide-open eyes and mouths agape.

"Jeez," Daniel said. I'm just funnin' you dudes."

The guys all sat around in Daniel's elegant living room, and together they righted all the wrongs of the world. Then it was time to say good night and all departed except Joey. He hung back to help Daniel clean up the evenings frolicking.

"So why haven't you married, Danny? You make enough money to be able to support a family in righteous luxury. Will no chick have you?" Joey queried.

"No, it's not that. I have had a few lady friends over the years, but I suppose the love bug has not ever taken the time to bite me. Yes, I do wish to fall in love, marry, and have children, but I'm in no rush to do so.

"But the story about my skateboard accident keeps coming up in my thoughts. You've told me over and over about how I bashed my head on the sidewalk and was knocked out, and I believe you. Also, one day I spoke with Mrs. Riley about it. I waited several weeks before I went to talk with her because I didn't know how to explain the hair and absent stitches. She told me that she did not see me eat sidewalk but she did go look at me and then called 911. The other guys that were there with us saw me knocked out and bleeding. The ambulance crew saw me, the hospital people saw me, the doctor and nurse who sewed me up saw me. My father and mother saw me before the shaving and stitches.

"The hospital lab tests confirmed beyond a doubt that the blood on the bandages was mine and the DNA matched. So what's the story, Joey? How did all this happen to me? Something happened to me to make all of this possible, but what? The whole thing was so fantastic that everyone at the hospital agreed that it was a huge mystery. Unexplainable. So all the hospital staff agreed to just sweep it under the table as if it never happened.

"But we know differently, don't we? It did, my lifetime friend, indeed happen. So how and why did it all disappear? At night when I am alone and all is quiet, my mind wonders to a place that I can never determine because nothing is clear and focused. I can never get a grasp as to where I am and then it all goes away.

"Besides that, Joey, my life could not be better, happier, or more fulfilled and precious. But something did happen to me, Joey, somewhere at sometime. I have a strong feeling that someone did at one time put a hand on my head and ruffle my hair. That someone, I think, was more than angel."

ABOUT THE AUTHOR

I was born in Fromberg, Montana.

After graduation from high school I joined the U.S. Navy and gave them 10 years.

The last two served in Chu Lai, Vietnam- 1968 & 69. Left the Navy, went to work and to collage and then found a career with Farmer's Insurance as a claims representative.

At age 48 I joined the U.S. Army Reserves and gave them 2 years.

Then I joined the U.S. Air Force Reserves and gave them 10 years.

I retired from the Military in 2000 and then from Farmer's Ins. In 2001.

I reside in the Pacific Northwest.

I had to live my life as it came. Adventure and misadventure, one step forward and one step back.

A laugh here and a sob there, but I wish I had lived it from the start as a writer.

Jesse Edward Corralez

Printed in the United States
By Bookmasters